RUTHLESS MATE

THE MARKED DRAGON PRINCE TRILOGY

JEN L. GREY

CHAPTER ONE

THE LUMP in my throat was so bulky, I couldn't swallow. I placed one hand on the back of the black leather sofa and ran the other down my stomach, where it hit the black belt of my short polka-dotted dress. I couldn't fathom what might be so urgent that Drake Hale, heir to a billion-dollar company, would show up *here* at eight on a Friday night.

I'd arrived home in Asheville, North Carolina, just an hour ago to stay for a few weeks before starting med school at UNC this summer, and he'd come knocking about fifteen minutes ago. I'd let him in and pointed to the door that led to the finished basement where my stepdad's office was.

My twin half siblings didn't even glance up from whatever video game they were playing. I hadn't gotten more than a *hi* from them since getting back, which... wasn't abnormal.

Eva punched the buttons on her controller harder than necessary, a victorious grin spreading across her face. A lock of dark brown hair fell over the back of her white strapless shirt, and her steel blue eyes narrowed. "I told you I'd learned some things since the last time we played."

"I see that." Elliott scowled. The only difference between them appearance-wise was that he was male and a little taller. Also, his hair was shorter, but it still hung in his eyes. Everything else about them was like looking into a mirror. "How the hell is that possible? We just played a few nights ago."

"Where there's a will, there's a way," she sang as she continued to press the buttons on the controller.

If I left, I was certain neither of them would notice. "Aren't you at all curious why a certain visitor is here?" I asked.

"Not at all." Elliott leaned forward on the sofa, focusing on the flat-screen TV hanging on the dark gray wall. "The few times I saw him at Dad's office, he made me uncomfortable, so my motto is 'stay the fuck away.'"

"Elliott," I hissed. "Language." Before Mom passed away six years ago, she'd asked me to watch over the twins. She'd said she hated putting the burden on me, but she had no one else to ask since my stepdad had begun acting strangely. So here I was, trying to make her proud.

However, I couldn't stop wondering why the owner of the largest rental property company, whose assets my stepfather managed as part of his realty business, was visiting this late on a Friday night.

"Oh, please, Ev." Eva rolled her eyes but kept her attention glued to the game. "We're eighteen. We can totally cuss."

My heart panged. They were growing up quickly, and every passing year was another reminder of how long Mom had been gone. God, I missed her. She'd wanted me to change the world with my love of painting and art, but when cancer had stolen the only parent I'd ever known, I'd decided to change the world in a different way—through medicine. I didn't want another kid to lose a parent to this horrible disease. It had left me an orphan and my half siblings with only one parent.

Something boomed from downstairs, and the walls shook all the way up to the living room.

My lungs seized. That was *definitely* something. But the twins kept playing their game as if they hadn't noticed a thing.

Figures. This was another thing I'd have to deal with on my own.

I marched toward the white-framed door in the middle of the wall behind me. My black strappy heels clacked on the white oak floors as I walked past the sizable kitchen on the right.

As I put a hand on the doorknob, a deep, angry voice stopped me in my tracks. "Did you really think we wouldn't find out about what *you* did, Peter?" It was Drake. The man emanated power even when he wasn't speaking.

Peter had been Mom's husband, and he'd allowed me to live under this roof after she'd died. I couldn't stand idly by while Drake attacked him.

I inhaled deeply, straightened my shoulders, and cracked open the oak door. As quietly as possible, I slipped down a few of the dark gray carpeted steps and peeked into the basement.

My world tilted.

Drake stood behind my stepdad's cherrywood desk, leaning his more than seven-foot-tall frame over my stepdad in his leather desk chair, which had crashed into the white wall behind him. Drake's formidable muscles were evident through his black suit, and his onyx eyes narrowed as he grasped the black armrests. Despite the turmoil, his brown-black hair remained perfectly in place, styled upward in small spikes, and his olive complexion glowed. He was the most handsome man I'd ever seen, but even when he wasn't furious, something about him unsettled me.

My stepdad's bottom lip quivered, and the crow's feet lining his chestnut eyes deepened. I could've sworn more gray had appeared at the temples of his light brown hair. I hadn't seen him since Christmas, when I'd come home to visit.

"I...I'm sorry." My stepdad's voice quivered. "I wasn't thinking."

"Clearly," Drake rasped, and his hand flinched like he wanted to hit my stepdad.

Two men in suits stood behind Drake with their arms crossed. They were slightly shorter than their boss but still taller than most men I'd encountered.

They were ganging up on my stepdad, and someone had to interfere.

Without thinking it through, I continued to the bottom of the stairs and cleared my throat loudly. "What's going on here?"

Drake's head spun toward me, and for a second, I swore his pupils elongated like a lizard's.

I gasped and shook my head. I had to be seeing things. His eyes were dark; it had to be a trick of the light.

"Dammit, Everly," my stepdad snapped. "You're always sticking your nose in places it doesn't belong."

My head jerked back like he'd slapped me. Here I was, trying to *help* him, and he was scolding me. Obviously, I'd messed up and needed to fix it.

"Sorry." I grimaced. I hated how weak I sounded. I'd always hoped he'd be like the dad I never had. "I thought I heard something, and I—"

"No, it's fine." A casual smile slipped over Drake's face as he straightened. He adjusted his black tie, which hadn't been out of place, and winked. "We are disagreeing over a business matter. I didn't mean to alarm you."

With his easygoing persona in place, I almost doubted what I'd walked in on, but I'd seen the conflict with my own eyes. I wasn't stupid. However, after Mom had died, I'd learned how to act myself, so I smiled back. "Well, misunderstandings happen. Don't they?"

He smirked and scanned me from head to toe before turning back to my stepdad. "Peter, you have three days to fix this in one of the two ways of which I've informed you. That's more than generous, based on the amount of time you've already had to remedy the situation. If you can't deliver, you know what will become rightfully mine."

My stepdad's Adam's apple bobbed, and he blanched.

The hairs on the nape of my neck rose. One thing was clear: the "situation" was bad, and it didn't take my perfect GPA to pick up on that.

Drake's gaze landed on me again, and he slightly bowed his head. "We'll leave now."

I nodded back. I needed to know what was going on, pronto, so I could fix it. Drake's family was the most powerful in our city. They owned most of downtown and so much more than I could even fathom, so I had to play nice.

I managed to spit out the one word I could say. "Goodbye."

My voice sounded rough, as if I hadn't drunk water in

days.

"Don't worry. We're going." Drake strode around the desk, then passed me and went up the stairs, each step steady and confident. I shrank back. He oozed dominance, and his aura struck me as unbalanced.

His men followed. The thicker guard, who resembled an MMA fighter, glared at me as he went by. His cobalt irises would have been mesmerizing if it hadn't been for the scowl on his face.

I listened carefully once all three of them were upstairs. When their footsteps didn't pause and the front door opened and closed, I let out a breath I hadn't realized I was holding.

Now that we were alone, I turned back to my stepdad. "What was that all about?"

He yanked on his button-down shirt, trying to smooth out the wrinkles, but I noted the dark blue spots where sweat had pooled under his arms. He scoffed. "It's none of your concern, Everly. Why are you even here?"

I flinched. I'd come downstairs to check on him, and that was the thanks I got? "I took my last exam at UNC and drove straight here. Thought I'd stay for the couple of weeks between now and the summer semester. I wanted to see my brother and sister." I kicked at the concrete floor, hating the way I explained myself to him all the time.

"You could've called them." He stood and rolled his chair back to the desk.

I called at least once a week, and half the time, they didn't answer. But I didn't want to get into that with him. I'd made a promise to Mom, and I intended to keep it. "It's not the same." He was deflecting, and I couldn't allow that. "Again, what was that about?"

"It's *business*. Part of *my family business*, which you *aren't* part of. You aren't my blood." He pointed to the stairs. "Now, I have a pressing issue to deal with. If you must stay, then stay in the guest room, and keep out of the way."

The guest room. That burned. It had been my room, but as soon as I'd moved into my dorm at UNC Chapel Hill, he'd taken it over and thrown my stuff away like I was a nuisance he'd gotten rid of.

"Peter—" I started.

He lifted a hand. "Seriously. I don't have time for this. Your sister's future is in my hands."

I froze. My sister? What did Eva have to do with his meeting with Drake? "Is that what Mr. Hale was talking about?"

"For fuck's sake, Everly." His nostrils flared. "Get out of my hair. Now."

My eyes burned. I should've known he wouldn't talk with me, but I'd hoped he might see that I could help him work out the problem. "Fine. Just let me know—"

"Leave!" he shouted and slammed his hands on the desk.

Any sense of dignity I had left was gone, but I refused to leave like a coward. Instead, I lifted my chin and slowly walked back upstairs.

With every step, my heart pounded harder. I worried that whatever had happened had endangered my sister, but that made no sense. Neither twin worked for my stepdad.

When I reached the top of the stairs, I went into the kitchen. With the open floor plan, I could see Eva and Elliott still engaged in their video game as if nothing had happened.

I wished I could be so oblivious.

I rushed past the rectangular white oak dining table that sat close to the windows and snatched my car keys off the cream-colored granite countertop of the cherrywood island marking the entryway into the kitchen. The cabinets and countertops matched throughout the room, and a glossy baby blue backsplash gave the space a modern edge.

Mom and I had picked out this kitchen when she'd been diagnosed with cancer. She'd wanted to do something special with me since I was losing my last parent, and she'd wanted this house to feel like home to me even after she was gone.

The familiar twinge of hurt zapped me, but I blinked hard, regaining focus. If Peter wouldn't tell me, then I had to find Drake to determine what was going on.

Marching past the sofa to the front door, I said, "I'm heading out for a little while."

Neither of the twins responded, as if I weren't even there. Like I was invisible.

As I stepped onto the long porch, the chill of twilight caused me to shiver. I should've grabbed a sweater on my way out, but I didn't want to waste time going back for one. I scurried to my white Audi A4 and slid into the black leather driver's seat.

If Drake had stayed around town, there was one place I could likely find him. He owned Dragon Alley in downtown Asheville, a luxury bar frequented by the city's elite and a handful of residents who were splurging for a special occasion. My stepdad had mentioned it when I was in town for Christmas.

Luckily, it was only a ten-minute drive away.

When I pulled up at the bar, I found a metered spot

nearby. On a Friday night downtown, most people would want more than one hour's time, but that would be plenty for me.

I paid for the meter on my phone and climbed out of the car. As I shut my door, a pleasant, almost tickly sensation ran down my back. I glanced around, my gaze drawn to a black sedan two parking spots down on my side of the street. A man sat in the vehicle, his gorgeous sky blue eyes on me. His baseball cap and the dim streetlights cast his face in shadow, but those eyes gleamed in the dark like beacons. From what I could tell, he was very attractive.

Everly! Get a grip. I couldn't believe I was standing here like a crazy person when I had to figure out what was going on with my stepdad and, more importantly, my sister. Forcing my attention off him, I walked to the thick wooden door that had the bar's name written on it in an elegant script.

Before I could reach the handle, a young man dressed in a black button-down shirt and slacks, who I hadn't even noticed standing there, opened the door. He smiled. "Welcome to Dragon Alley."

I walked into the most whimsical bar I'd ever seen. The floor was hardwood, each board alternating between dark and light. The bar and tables were made of a coffee-stained wood, and the underside of the crowded main bar was lit with warm, yellow-toned lights. The overhead lighting was perfect, neither too bright nor too dark, but rather the sort of soft illumination that felt like an invitation to curl up and read one of my favorite contemporary romances. Varying shades of brown bricks accented the walls. The low hum of intimate conversations and soft jazz music added to the ambiance.

Unsurprisingly, there were no open seats. Even

though everyone was dressed up, the place was trendy and welcoming.

Drake and his two shadows were sitting in the back at a corner table away from everyone else.

Even as the weight lifted from my shoulders, something hard settled in my stomach. Panic, maybe?

"If you'd like a drink, you can wait—" the host started.

But I had no desire to listen. Instead, I marched toward the person I'd come here to see.

"Ma'am!" the host called after me. "You can't go back there."

Like hell I couldn't. Drake might be rich and influential, but he couldn't just barge into my stepdad's house and threaten him, especially if that threat involved my sister.

Drake sat at the end of the table, facing the door. His attention locked on me, and he said something, causing his two shadows, who were facing him, to look over their shoulders at me.

Arching a brow, Drake tilted his head, observing.

As I grew closer, something inside me urged me to turn around and run. But that wouldn't get me any answers.

I stopped at their table and placed one hand on my hip.

"Ma'am!" the host exclaimed. "This is the owner's private—"

"Leave her," Drake commanded as he ran a hand along his chin. "She can stay."

Footsteps hurried away as the host left us.

"Sir," the cobalt-eyed man said.

"Falkor, Ladon, get us a round from the bar." Drake motioned for them to go.

Jaws twitching, the two men growled but obeyed, leaving Drake and me alone.

"How can I help you?" Drake placed his hands on the table.

"Tell me what that was about back at the house with my stepdad." I tensed as every cell in my body told me to run.

He chuckled humorlessly. "Your *stepdad* embezzled from my company. He hasn't deposited all the cash payments from the tenants for a few years now, and he needs to pay me back the missing money or provide something of equal value."

My stomach roiled. "My *sister*? What are you going to do? Pimp her out?" I clenched my hands, ready to punch the smirk off his face.

"Of course not. It's hard to find women who aren't after my money. Your sister has the proper status and education to suit my...specific needs. We'll be legally united with no way to sever ties." Drake tapped his fingers on the table. "She'll never want for anything, and she'll bear the heirs I need to carry on my legacy."

My sister would be forced to marry this man and have his children as repayment for my stepdad's crime? That was disgusting. "How much does he owe you?"

"One million dollars. Give or take." He grabbed the half glass of brown liquid sitting in front of him and drained it, his eyes remaining locked on me.

I inhaled. My mother's dying wish replayed in my head. I couldn't abandon my sister to that fate. There had to be another way out of this situation; it wasn't Eva's penance to bear.

"Take me in her place."

CHAPTER TWO

HE CHOKED and coughed as he placed the glass on the table a little too hard, trying to play off his shock. Then he cleared his throat and blinked a few times, his angular face somehow appearing sharper. "You want to take your sister's place and be at my beck and call?"

When he put it that way, it sounded even worse. That one phrase exposed what marriage to him would be like: being controlled. But my sister had turned eighteen last month, in April. She deserved to go to college and enjoy this time of her life. Though I was supposed to start my formal premed education in two weeks, I'd had four years of college and graduated with a bachelor's degree. I'd had more time to live—granted, I'd spent most of my time, including weekends, either studying or working at a local coffee shop, but at least I'd had the choice.

I straightened my shoulders. "I'm not kidding. The offer is sincere. I'm older, and..." Spilling my heart out to anyone, let alone a peculiar, good-looking man, wasn't something I was comfortable with. I sighed. "Does it matter why? Besides, you should know that Eva and

Elliott are twins and very close. If you take one, the other will be there all the time." Maybe if I focused on him having a frequent visitor, it would sway him to my side.

Pursing his lips, he rubbed his finger along the rim of his glass and stared into space as if he were deliberating. Finally, he exhaled. "I hadn't considered that. But won't they do the same for you?" He observed me.

The question was legitimate, but it felt like he'd stabbed me in the heart. My throat went dry, and I tried to school my expression. I wanted to lie, but I suspected it wouldn't do me any favors. If I wanted him to trust me, I had to be honest. "No, they won't. Though I believe my siblings care about me, we aren't close. If I didn't come home, I would never see them."

He steepled his fingers and tapped them against his lips. "And your father wouldn't—"

"*Step*father," I interjected. I didn't want him to get confused about my relationship with Peter. He was the only parental figure I had, but he was upfront about not wanting me to view him that way. "And he doesn't care about me." I cringed. Maybe I should've left that last part out. If taking my sister was a way of collecting the million Peter had embezzled, then Drake might be seeking someone Peter cared about as punishment.

"This gets more interesting." He scratched at his scruff. "How old are you?"

I wasn't sure how that was relevant. He was drinking at a bar, so we were close enough in age that it shouldn't matter, but I didn't want to risk sounding ornery. "Twenty-two."

He smirked. "An older woman by a year."

My blood turned cold. He was truly considering this, which was what I wanted, but it also terrified me. Though

I didn't want Eva trapped in that situation, I didn't want to be, either.

But I'd made a promise.

Dropping his forearms onto the table, he nodded. "In a way, it's better that you're volunteering. We're closer in age, and you seem more mature, seeing as your nose isn't shoved in some video game." He rolled his eyes. "I won't have to contend with a disgruntled teenager who pouts about being locked in with me or visiting family since you're estranged. You'll be all *mine*, which is exactly what I want."

He stood, and I took a step back. I didn't want us to be too close, which, given the circumstances and the offer I'd made him, was somewhat ironic, but I didn't know him. My gut screamed that the more I learned about him, the more I'd dislike him. Though he was attractive, he was intense in a disturbing kind of way. There was something animalistic and raw about him, like a predator circling its prey. Unfortunately, I was that prey.

Placing a finger under my chin, he tipped my face up.

His pupils slitted as he surveyed me from my face to my toes.

I swallowed hard. That was the second time they'd done that. But when I blinked and looked again, his eyes were normal.

The stress of exams, missing my graduation next weekend, and coming back here where Mom's memory haunted me even more must have been getting to me.

He nodded. "Your face is symmetrical. Your light gray eyes are alluring. And your full rosy lips will make many men jealous of me."

Then he turned my head to one side and the other, evaluating my profile.

My skin crawled. I felt like an animal in a show. I couldn't believe he was judging my attributes as if I had no feelings. My hands clenched, ready to punch the jerk in the face, but I couldn't. Then he would take my sister.

He continued without a pause, "Your fair skin is a little much, but we can fix that. Your alignment and body shape are sufficient, though I don't much like the golden shade of your hair. Still, the length and fullness are adequate."

Heart pounding, I swallowed the anger swirling inside me. I'd inherited my golden hair from Mom, and I wasn't willing to change it, not even for him. "Thanks for listing all my pros and cons." I couldn't hide my disgust.

"Watch that tone, *dear*. After all, you came here looking for me." He smirked and dipped his head closer.

This guy was a narcissistic asshole, but he had all the control, and he knew it. Stomach souring, I swallowed again as bile inched up my throat.

He dropped his hand and nodded. "Overall, I suppose you're pretty enough, and with my dominant features, my heirs will stand apart from all others." He held out a hand. "I accept your offer. You'll be picked up in three days, as I informed Peter. After all, I *am* a man of my word."

I'd heard rumors of his arrogance among some of the people in the city. How their rent would increase, and Drake would laugh when they complained, asking what they were going to do about it.

I'd assumed they were making him out to be more villainous than he was, especially since he was so young, but now I was certain they hadn't made Drake sound horrible enough.

"That's only *if* we don't come up with the money."

He was acting as if there weren't an alternative, but I wouldn't just hand over my freedom without a fight.

His dark eyes lightened with mirth. "Of course, darling."

The back of my throat burned. He enjoyed making others feel inadequate.

There was no way I could marry him.

"Good." I straightened my back and shook his hand, sealing the deal. As soon as I could, I released him and pivoted toward the door. "I'd better get to work."

He grabbed my arm, jerking me back toward him. His fingers dug into my skin. The urge to get out of his grip was damn near uncontrollable, but I had to be complacent, or he might change his mind.

"I want to be clear. If you plan on keeping our agreement, make sure you don't do something disgusting and soil the goods." He waved a hand from my mouth to my crotch, his insinuation clear. "I won't accept someone who sleeps with people for money. I don't share what's *mine*. Do you understand?"

My cheeks burned. "Isn't that what you're forcing either my sister or me to do?" I wasn't good at keeping my mouth shut when I was angry. Since Mom's death, I tried to let Peter's indifference and the twins' obliviousness roll off my back. I didn't want to alienate myself from my family more than I already was. If I stood up to my stepdad and became too much of a nuisance, I wouldn't be welcomed back. So, for the most part, I took it.

But I'd just learned that I had my limits.

"No, *darling*." He lowered his mouth to my ear, his hot breath hitting the sensitive shell. "You'll be treated like a princess. It's not the same, so don't try to cheapen it."

I shivered, but it wasn't from desire. I wanted to get away from him. "That thought hadn't crossed my mind."

His grip went slack, and the blood rushed down my arm, causing it to tingle, but his mouth stayed right next to my ear. "That's a good girl."

Something was seriously wrong with him. I had to leave before I did something I regretted in the morning. "I'll get Peter to contact you when we get the money." I inhaled as I walked toward the door, refusing to look back. I was certain I *would* vomit if I did.

"Remember, three days, darling," he cooed, then broke out in loud laughter.

It was the last thing I heard before the bar door whooshed shut behind me, chilling me to the core.

I rushed to my car, shaking from the meeting. There was something sinister about Drake, and it unnerved me.

As I approached my vehicle, I looked for the man with striking blue eyes, but the spot where he'd been parked was empty.

Somehow, that chilled me even more.

The three days passed more quickly than I'd thought possible. I stood in the center of the *guest bedroom*, taking a deep breath as the realization of my horrible situation sank in.

I'd painted until my wrists had flared up with tendonitis and then painted some more. I hadn't completed a single painting since Mom had passed, but in the past three days, I'd done six detailed and intricate pieces and rushed to the local gallery to offer them for sale. Luckily, they'd honored my previous agreement without hesitation since I'd sold several paintings through them while I was in high school. They'd reached out to me several times after Mom's death because a customer had asked for more of my artwork, so I could only hope the customers were still interested.

Mom had loved my portraits of downtown Asheville and my landscapes of the woods and mountains that surrounded our city. I'd been painting since I was quite young, and I'd earned money for college and a reputation locally for my work. I should've been able to sell these pieces for decent money, but the inquiring customer hadn't dropped by, and no one else had purchased them yet.

Between that and driving for Uber at night, I had hoped to come up with a portion of the payment to help my stepdad with the total, but as soon as Drake had informed him that he had switched plans to me, my stepdad hadn't even tried to repay him.

No wonder Drake had laughed so hard when I'd left the bar.

I stood at the window next to the black, iron-framed queen-size bed. The window overlooked the driveway where Drake would be pulling up any second.

Each heartbeat was a stark reminder that I was closer to losing my freedom. I wasn't sure what to expect once I left here, but I was certain I would lose touch with the twins. At least it was because I was fulfilling my promise to Mom.

Tearing my gaze from the view, I walked halfway through the wide-open attic room with its slanted ceiling. It was one of the largest bedrooms in the house, but there was no connecting bathroom or closet. I suspected that was why I'd received it when we'd moved in with Peter.

I walked to one wall and touched the light blue paint. Underneath my fingertips, I could feel the slight indentations of what Peter had covered up—the painting Mom and I had done together when we'd moved in and made the room mine.

My heart fractured from the bittersweet memories. God, how I missed her.

An engine rumbled below, and my lungs seized. I didn't bother checking the window because I heard two car doors open.

Drake was here to collect his *property*.

Me.

I exhaled, forcing myself to breathe. Passing out wouldn't accomplish anything.

With more self-control than I'd believed possible, I strolled to the bed and picked up the two dark duffel bags of belongings I'd brought back from college. It was everything I owned, and it had been hard to realize that my life could be packed up so easily.

The doorbell rang, and I turned around in the room, giving it one final look. Despite the agony cutting through my chest, I pulled up the memory of what the room had looked like with the mural Mom and I had created—a sunrise over downtown Asheville in front of Mom's and my favorite coffee spot.

"Everly!" Eva yelled, her voice sounding strange. "You have a visitor."

If only it were a visitor and not my new "owner."

Part of me wished I hadn't left campus early and skipped my graduation ceremony. Then I wouldn't be in this predicament. But Eva would be. I had to remember that.

I glanced at the bracelet on my wrist, a gift from my

mother. She'd given it to me the day she married Peter, a reminder of what I meant to her. I hadn't worn it since she'd passed, the memories stinging and too fresh, but today, I needed it. I needed her. It was white gold and formed with interchanging small hearts and diamonds, with two bigger hearts hanging down and inscribed with *Everly* and *The love between a mother and daughter is forever*.

My eyes burned with tears.

"Everly!" my stepdad yelled.

Blowing out a breath, I opened the door. I knew better than to delay the inevitable. It only made things harder. I walked downstairs, each step slow and steady, and when the front door came into view, I stopped, surprised.

Drake wasn't there.

Instead, it was the same two guards who had shadowed Drake the other day, plus a tall, beautiful girl I'd never seen before.

She lifted a brow as her mocha eyes examined me. Long, curly, dark brown hair flowed over her shoulders and stopped midway down her back. Where Drake had pointed out that I was pale, she was the opposite—a gorgeous bronze. She stood about two inches taller than my stepdad, bringing her in at around six feet. Her height only added to her allure.

My five-foot-eight height made me taller than most girls, but now I felt short.

The girl glanced back at the guards. "Not what I was expecting, but it makes sense."

"Does it?" Falkor grumbled.

I wasn't sure how to take that, but I didn't give a damn.

"Hi, Everly." The beautiful girl turned back toward

me. "I'm Saphira. Drake couldn't come to pick you up today, so I'm here in his place."

That was more than okay with me. I nodded, not trusting myself to talk.

"Take her bags and go upstairs to get whatever else she needs," Saphira ordered the two men.

Falkor took the two duffel bags out of my hands as Ladon stepped toward the stairs.

"No need. This is all of it." I cleared my throat.

Both twins stood by the couch, watching everything. My stepdad was at the door, holding it open.

Saphira's head tilted back, but then she shook it. "No worries. You'll have more than you'll ever want or need once we get you to your new home."

"Her home?" Elliott crossed his arms. "Her home's here. What are you talking about?"

I hadn't told them anything. Partly because I was a coward and didn't know what to say, and partly because they'd been busy the past few days, and I hadn't seen them.

"Your sister's future is with Drake Hale, and she's moving in with him." My stepdad seemed jovial. "This is a very good thing for our family."

No, it was a very good thing for *him*. He was the reason I was in this mess.

"Wait. That seems fast." Eva bit her bottom lip. "I didn't realize you and Drake were dating. Of course we'll come visit."

"That will be up to Drake," Saphira interjected.

As expected, he was going to remove the last members of my family from my life. My shoulders shook, but I couldn't fall apart.

"But—" Eva started.

"You heard her." Peter waved his hand, telling me to leave. "We aren't invited, and Drake is waiting for her. We don't want to hold her up."

"We do need to go." Ladon returned to the door. "Drake will be waiting."

I was sure he would be.

Saphira, Ladon, and Falkor walked out the door, and I followed, each step harder than the last. I was heading toward a future I didn't want, and I was at the mercy of fate.

As I turned to the twins to say goodbye, I was surprised to find them right behind me. They pulled me into a group hug.

"Be careful, E," Eva whispered.

I hadn't been prepared for concern. They must have sensed something was wrong. I returned their embrace, taking a deep breath and committing their scents and how they felt to memory. Then I pulled myself away before I couldn't.

"Hurry up," my stepdad gritted. As soon as I stepped onto the porch, Peter said, "It's about time she was useful." Then the front door slammed shut.

What was left of my heart shattered, and I couldn't even feel my legs as I made my way to the black sedan. Falkor held the door open, and I slid into the leather back seat, next to Saphira.

She frowned. "I'm sorry your stepdad is an asshole. No wonder you're here."

Out of everyone I knew, she was the one who'd understood in seconds what people who'd seen my relationship with Peter for years had never picked up on—he didn't treat me like a daughter.

Afraid to speak, I only nodded. I couldn't risk breaking into tears.

The car pulled away, and I laid my head on the headrest. I didn't need to watch the city pass by. Memories of Mom haunted me, and every mile toward the mountainous outskirts of the city only added to the pain. That had probably been the last time I'd ever see my brother and sister.

After we'd driven for twenty minutes, Falkor shouted, "Holy fuck!"

CHAPTER THREE

MY EYES FLEW OPEN, and I inhaled sharply. I glanced around, searching for the other vehicle with which we surely had to be on a collision course, but all I saw was the empty two-lane road leading us into the isolated peaks of the Blue Ridge Mountains.

"Brace yourselves!" Falkor yelled, and clutched the steering wheel hard enough that his knuckles blanched.

He was frantic, but there was *nothing* on the road. We were surrounded by freshly sprouted trees.

Following Ladon's focus to our right, I squinted into the trees. Something barreled toward us.

I gasped.

It was too big to be a bullet.

I yelped as Saphira grabbed my shoulders and pushed my upper body out of view of the side window.

Instead of a crashing noise, something thumped outside our car.

"Dammit, the tire blew," Falkor gritted.

"Keep driving!" Ladon exclaimed.

I tried to sit upright, but Saphira shoved me down

again. Her strength was remarkable, even for her larger stature.

My back ached from crouching over my knees, but I supposed that was a better alternative to dying.

The car jerked, indicating the tire had deflated. We could drive for a while on the rim, but I wasn't sure for how long. Every few seconds, the vehicle would lurch, forcing Falkor to slow down.

Ladon growled, "Here comes another fucking arrow. What year is this person living in? The Middle Ages? Use a damn gun!"

A second thump told me everything I needed to know. Another tire had been blown, and it sounded like it was the one right behind me. Robin Hood was attacking us. That was the only rational explanation I could come up with.

"We have to stop," Falkor said with disgust. "Whoever is attacking us will catch up, so it's better if we get out and prepare to fight."

These guys were idiots. Yes, we were moving slowly for a car, but we were going at least twenty miles per hour. No person could catch up with us at that speed. "Just keep going!"

Saphira exhaled. "We would if that were an option."

Lovely, she was on the same page as these morons. We were going to die. Granted, if we drove far enough, we'd get out of range of the archer, and if we kept a steady pace to God knew where, we might make it out of this alive.

"I want it noted that I believe this is a horrible idea," I said as I sat up again.

Saphira glared at me, but if we were climbing out of the car, there was no reason for me to hide.

The two men opened their doors. Falkor called over his shoulder, "You two stay inside. We'll eliminate the threat and go from there." He slammed his door shut.

I detested their sexist manner, but I remained silent. Though I disliked their arrogant implication that two women couldn't fight, for myself, I couldn't disagree. I'd dedicated my life to improving my painting techniques and studying. Self-defense hadn't been part of that program, and just ten minutes on an elliptical kicked my ass.

I rolled my eyes. "We should've kept *driving*."

"Falkor and Ladon are highly skilled warriors trained to assess danger." Saphira leaned forward to look out my window. "If they say this is the best option, it is, even if we don't understand it."

Of course she would take their side. She was with them. The best thing I could do was remain silent and pray their stupidity didn't kill us.

I pulled out my cell phone and dialed 911, one of the first things people trained to react to dangerous situations would do.

"What are you doing?" Saphira asked as the phone rang.

"Calling for help, since no one else is." For six years, I'd had to shut down my attitude and behave. In the past three days, that control had been ruined, all due to my affiliation with Drake. My future wasn't looking very promising.

She snatched the phone from my hand and pressed the red button, cutting off the line. "We are *not* calling for help. Falkor and Ladon have it covered."

Great, she was an idiot, too. Maybe this was par for the course with all people tied to Drake.

A loud roar shook the car, and my heart jumped into my throat. I turned to my window.

My entire world stopped...because what I saw was impossible.

It only existed in fiction.

A huge, shimmery plum dragon flew by the car toward the warriors. Its scales were the very color I favored when painting the night sky.

I froze, unable to do anything but gape.

This had to be a dream—no, a nightmare. Maybe this situation with Drake and my time back in Asheville was an elaborate anxiety dream fueled by my exams.

That was the only plausible explanation.

Doing what I'd seen countless people do in television shows and movies, I pinched my arm.

The sharp sting forced my lungs to expel air, and I couldn't mask my grunt. *Ow. That hurt.*

"What are you *doing*?" Saphira scoffed. "I don't think bruising yourself will make the dragon go away."

Her confirmation of what I'd seen didn't make me feel better. In fact, my vision blurred as the car seemed to close in on me, suffocating me.

"Dra...gon?" I gasped, hoping that saying the word would make sense of everything.

It didn't.

The world spun, and I reached forward to steady myself.

"Everly!" Saphira shouted...or I thought she did. However, noises were gurgling as if I were under water.

Something hard smacked me on the cheek, and the world righted itself as my skin stung.

"Listen to me. I need you to stay focused. That dragon is after something, and I'm not sure what."

Her face twisted in anger. "We may have to run for it."

Falkor and Ladon stood beside the car, ready to face down a *dragon*.

I reached for the handle to open my door. "They need to get back inside the car!" But my hand stilled as Falkor's clothes ripped from his body and yellow-green splotches dotted his skin, becoming what could only be described as scales.

My mind turned to mush. This *had* to be a dream. But as I kept my eyes on Falkor, his body quadrupled in size, and wings sprouted from his back. He flapped his wings and soared toward the silvery plum dragon.

As he rushed our attacker, I shook my head, ready to open the door again to get Ladon inside, but then *he* began transforming, too. Pine green scales covered his body as his black suit ripped to shreds and fell off him.

No wonder Saphira had trusted them to handle the situation. But that didn't comfort me. I'd been riding around with *dragons* without a clue. What else didn't I know about what I'd signed up for?

"Shit!" Saphira exclaimed, bringing me back to the present.

I followed her gaze in time to watch the gorgeous silver-plum dragon breathe fire at Falkor, who darted below the stream, dodging the flames. As he shot upward, the dragon swung around and used his long, thick tail to smack Falkor in the head.

Falkor dropped, but the dragon didn't let up. He darted after him, and as Falkor regained his balance and flapped his wings, the dragon bit into Falkor's shoulder. He threw his head back and roared in pain.

Now that Ladon was fully shifted, he soared toward

his friend. Smoke trickled from his nose, conveying his rage. I wasn't a dragon, but even I understood what was going on there.

Attacker Dragon released his hold on Falkor and shot up high enough to kick the dragon in the head. Falkor flew backward and rammed into the thick Fraser and balsam firs and red spruces. The earth shook, and the crash confirmed I wasn't imagining things.

Saphira was counting on them to protect us, but I didn't have the same good feeling about it. I cleared my throat and winced. The skin felt raw. "Isn't Falkor in charge?"

"Yeah, but Ladon is a strong fighter, too," Saphira said, then jumped over the center console into the front seat.

She wasn't growing scales...yet. "That's not reassuring!"

"I'm not trying to reassure you. You're a grown-ass woman. I'm just telling you what I know." She pressed the start button on the car and let out a huge sigh. "Thank gods he left the keys in the car. At least he was thinking on his feet."

"Or the keys dropped to the ground close to the car when he was, you know, becoming a *dragon*, and as soon as we drive too far, the car will stall." I didn't understand how she could remain so rational. We were under attack, and the *men* who were protecting us weren't even human. Maybe that should've been comforting, given our attacker wasn't, either, but it wasn't.

Saphira snarled in a way that wasn't *human*, and I sank into my seat.

"They're right here." She reached into the cup holder and lifted the black keys. "So you can stop being a drama queen and maybe yank that stick out of your ass." She shifted into gear and took off way faster than she should have with two blown tires.

Somehow, moving forward eased some of my anxiety. I recognized what this was—a false sense of security—but I'd take it.

I glanced out the back window to see Ladon and Attacker Dragon engaged in a battle. Instead of being on the defensive, Ladon was now the one landing blows.

Though I was petrified, watching Attacker Dragon fight was like watching an artist paint. He was skilled, and every movement flowed into the next, unlike Ladon, who struck fast and hard in spurts.

Attacker Dragon jerked his head to look at us. Smoke poured from his nose as he focused back on Ladon, barely ducking his head in time to avoid a strike of his front paw.

With Attacker Dragon's body not where Ladon had expected, Ladon's dragon form overshot and flew over Attacker Dragon. Attacker Dragon tilted his head back and blew fire at Ladon's underside.

Ladon released an ear-shattering screech, and I covered my ears to block out the cry. Attacker Dragon then slammed his chest and front claws into Ladon's burned stomach.

After being lifted at least fifty feet high, Ladon came crashing down. He moved his wings, trying to fly, but wasn't fast enough. As he barreled downward, Attacker Dragon spun and nailed him in the head. Ladon tumbled to the ground, meeting the same fate as his friend.

The car shook, and Saphira glanced into the rearview mirror, her face pale. "Please tell me that was the purple dragon and not Ladon."

"I could, but then I'd be *lying*." I ground my teeth,

sending a jolt of pain through my jaw. That was a sign that I was stressed out and needed to relax and get my emotions in check.

"Of course not. That would be too easy," she spat, and glanced out the window. "I can't see him from this angle."

I redirected my attention outside, and my heart dropped into my stomach. This day kept getting worse, but I'd bet we hadn't hit a low yet. "He won't be out of your sight for long." Attacker Dragon hurtled toward us. "Whatever he wants must be in this car."

She pressed the gas harder, and the car lurched even more.

Screw her. I leaned over and snatched my cell phone from where she'd placed it behind her. I dialed 911 again and placed the phone under my butt to muffle it.

"Everly, hang up the phone *now*," she commanded. "What are you going to say? A huge-ass dragon is chasing us?"

"No, I'm going to tell them we need help and we're driving on our rims like maniacs because someone is chasing us." The car shuddered from the flat tires, and my stomach jiggled nonstop. I could easily throw up. "Even if the dragon doesn't catch us, our vehicle could smash into a tree and leave no survivors. So, I'm sorry, but I want to live."

I could be snarky, too.

"Drake's going to *kill* me," she rasped. "But he'll be more upset if I don't get you to him in one piece."

That was an odd thing to say. I was certain Drake didn't care about me. He wanted me for babies and status, so it was what I could do for him that he wanted to protect.

But I'd take it.

I looked out the window again and yelped. Attacker Dragon had caught up to us, and his head was lowered so it was level with my door. Sky blue eyes focused on me with humanlike intelligence despite the elongated pupils. The eyes were bright, gleaming like those of the man I'd seen in the car outside the bar. My stomach tightened. If Falkor and Ladon were both human and dragon, it stood to reason this dragon was also human.

Something tugged inside me. My head screamed at me to move to the other side of the car, but I was helpless. All I could do was stare into the beast's mesmerizing eyes. Something about them called to the void inside me.

The dragon flew faster, and one of its large feet reached for the handle of my door.

Self-preservation kicked in *finally*. I flipped the lock and slid to the other side of the back seat. "It's trying to open my door!"

"I *told* Drake it was stupid to tell the entire château about you," she seethed. "Hold on tight. It's about to get rough." If *this* wasn't rough, I feared what was about to happen next.

Wait. Château?

The car lurched as she slammed on the brakes. The right side of the car skidded, and sparks shot upward from metal dragging on asphalt. She cut the wheel hard, and the sedan lifted to the left side as she spun the car in the opposite direction.

My body was jostled everywhere in the back seat, and I wished she'd been more explicit with her warning.

We barely missed the metal railing on the other side, and she pushed the gas hard again, racing back toward the city. This was a better strategy; we were no longer going up a freaking mountain, and we were probably closer to the city than wherever Drake lived.

The dragon roared behind us, and when the car settled, I turned around to see it had already eliminated the distance between us. It sped toward us, gaining despite our speed.

"It's—" I started, but the ceiling of the sedan made a sound like crumpling plastic. My head jerked upward. Talons had pierced the roof.

We weren't getting away.

CHAPTER FOUR

MY HEART RACED, and my ears rang like I'd just left a concert. I'd imagined myself in many different scenarios, but *this* had never crossed my mind.

Silver-plum scaly wings flanked the car, and the ceiling groaned as if the dragon had landed on it. I grabbed the headrest of Saphira's seat. "What do we do?" I tried to say, but barely any noise left my mouth.

"I don't *know*," she spat. "But I hear sirens. 911 must have traced your call."

Holy shit. She'd heard me. I wasn't sure how, but I already suspected she was one of *them*. They must have excellent hearing, or that was what the few books and movies about dragons I'd heard about portrayed. Now I sort of wished I'd enjoyed those stories like Mom had. Maybe then I'd have an idea about how to get out of this situation.

All I could do was focus. "That's good. We need help." I waved my arms around. "We're about to get smushed."

"Not *that* kind of help, Everly." She stomped on the

gas. The car lurched, and more sparks flew off the rims. Every few seconds, the car clunked as if we were rolling from rim to tire.

The ceiling caved in further as the dragon put more weight on it. Was he going to squash us alive?

"He wants something from one of us, so he won't *smush* us. And unless you consider flattening humans like pancakes a good thing, you've involved humans who will get hurt in the crossfire. This dragon won't give up until he gets what he wants, and humans can't find out about our kind." She glanced in the rearview mirror at me.

I hung my head. I hadn't considered that I might have sentenced the police to their demise. I'd been so stupid.

She slammed on the brakes, and I jerked forward. The downward right tilt of the car made it impossible to stay in place. A loud screeching noise came from the roof, and I steadied myself and glanced up as claws pierced it again. This car would soon be a convertible.

The *whoosh* of the flapping wings grew louder, and the sedan groaned as we were lifted off the ground.

I gulped.

Our attacker was strong enough to lift a fucking car.

Needing comfort, I ran my thumb over the bracelet Mom had given me. I had a feeling I'd be reuniting with her soon. I'd always hoped that when the time came, the idea of seeing her again would comfort me, but I didn't want to die. I had so much I wanted to do. I snorted. "At least the car's level now."

Saphira turned around and gaped. "Have you lost your damn mind?"

"Let's see." When I was stressed out, I made bad jokes. I could admit it wasn't one of my best attributes, but it was how I coped. "Until twenty minutes ago, I didn't even know *dragons* existed, and now I'm being carried off in a car by one. I'm going with yes, and I hope I wake up from this horrible nightmare, pronto. Someone must have drugged my coffee this morning."

"*This* isn't a bad trip." She leaned over and popped open the glove box. "This is your life since you agreed to be Drake's."

That was enough to slam my sanity back into me. I wanted to ask if he was a dragon, too, but I had a pretty good guess that he was, and I wasn't sure I could handle it if she confirmed my suspicion.

She reached inside and removed a black pistol. "Thank gods those two are always prepared."

If this dragon could pick up a car, I doubted that a gun would work on him. "Why don't you shift?" That made the most sense, given the situation.

"If you want to die, I can." She lowered the gun and moved like she was putting it into her pocket. "If I shift in here, I'll destroy the inside of the vehicle, including you. And if Falkor and Ladon couldn't take him in dragon form, I don't have much hope."

That was great. "You're not a warrior?"

"No, I'm not. Drake asked me to come and welcome you since he's dealing with a situation." She exhaled.

For some reason, even though she was a dragon, she didn't scare me. Not like our attacker and the other men.

I hated that she was in this mess because of me.

I glanced out the side window. The road was far below us, and I had no way of telling how high we were. I could see the flashing red and blue lights of the approaching police, but they were like tiny little toys. By the time they made it to where we were, we'd be out of sight.

I inched to the middle of the bench seat in the back and clutched the driver's and passenger's headrests. I wasn't sure what I feared more, the talons over my head or the possibility of the dragon releasing the car and us falling. Either way, I was terrified.

Saphira's brows furrowed. "Are you okay?"

I shook my head. I hadn't been this frightened since Mom had died, leaving me all alone.

"I'll do everything I can to protect you." Saphira placed a hand over her heart. "I promise."

I believed her, which was insane. Even though we'd known each other for less than an hour, she'd already proven she would follow through on that promise.

The car groaned and tilted forward slightly. The trees grew larger and the ground closer, and my mouth went dry.

"We're landing," Saphira said and rolled her shoulders. "Just...stay inside and let me handle this."

She was being vague, and there had to be a reason—the dragon overhearing, I assumed. If she could hear sirens from miles away, then the dragon could hear anything we said inside the car.

A shiver ran down my spine. I didn't like that thought *at all.*

The trees rushed toward us, and I closed my eyes. I clutched my bracelet with my free hand and focused on the last moment I'd shared with Mom before she was hospitalized. She'd been at home in her own bed, and we'd sipped on our favorite lattes while watching *I Am Dragon*, a movie she'd claimed was one of the most epic love stories of all time. *How ironic.* The woman in the movie had been kidnapped by a dragon.

Branches screeched against the glass, and my eyes flew open. We were almost to the ground.

The car shook on impact, and my head jerked back. Though it hadn't been a fast drop, the landing hadn't been graceful.

The dragon removed its talons from the top of the car, leaving holes in the roof. It lifted into the air and flew away to the right.

My breathing calmed. I whispered, "He's leaving."

Saphira glanced over her shoulder and rolled her eyes. "He wouldn't take us, then leave. He's likely shifting back into his human form. *That* must be his ride." She gestured to a black, four-seat ATV parked twenty feet from the car under a huge Fraser fir.

There went any sense of clarity I had. "Then we need to run *now*." If he was shifting, this could be the chance we needed. I pushed open my door and climbed out. My black, strappy high heels sank into the ground, and a twig scraped my ankle.

Son of a gun. That hurt.

Not a second later, Saphira got out of the car and glared at me. She mouthed, *What are you doing? I said stay in the car!*

I hated that I could make out her words. I would *not* just sit here and wait to be taken, killed, or tortured.

Ignoring her, I yanked off my high heels and tossed them back into the car. *There. One problem solved.*

Saphira stared at me as if I'd grown a second head. After today, I wouldn't count it as implausible.

I tiptoed around the vehicle, not making a single sound. Ha! Who said I couldn't make it outdoors? Mom had said I could do anything if I put my mind to it.

I was halfway to the ATV when a deep voice on my right called out, "What do you think you're doing?"

Placing my hands over my mouth, I held in my scream and pivoted toward the voice. Then my brain short-circuited.

It had to be the man from outside the bar because those eyes matched. I'd known he was attractive that night, but in full daylight, he was the sexiest man I'd ever seen. He stood about ten feet away from me, past the car. His medium-brown hair hung in his eyes, and his tan complexion made him look like a model. He was shirtless, and everywhere my gaze landed was full of muscles—all seven and a half feet of him. However, his eyes revealed everything I needed to know—this was the plum dragon that had attacked us.

Saphira pinched the bridge of her nose. "I believe she thinks she was being quiet."

His attention swung to her. "Well, she's not your problem anymore."

Alarms rang in my head, and shock had me at a loss for words. Why would someone like *him* try to kidnap me? I was no one of value. Hell, even my own stepdad had handed me over as if I were an object to be traded.

"Like *hell* she isn't." Saphira removed the pistol from her side and aimed it at our attacker. "*You* won't be my problem anymore." Her hand shook, but she pulled the trigger.

Our attacker spun around, and the bullet hit a spot five feet away from him. She would've barely nicked him if he hadn't moved.

He ran to the tree line and ducked behind a huge red spruce.

Keeping her focus on the spot where he'd disappeared, Saphira ran toward me and said, "Check to see if the key is in the ATV."

I stood there, unable to move.

"Everly!" she snapped as she caught up to me. "Do you *want* him to catch you?"

Even if the guy was drool-worthy, I didn't want to be forced to go somewhere against my will...again. Catering to Drake was enough.

My feet finally moved, my sense of self-preservation kicking back in. Thank goodness for that instinct.

I hurried to the ATV and leaned into the vehicle. My eyes burned. "They're not in here."

She growled. "Go to the back and get the VIN number off the ATV. It'll be on the bottom left."

I listened to what she said and found the tag. I rattled off the number to her, and she didn't even jot it down. "Do I need to find something—"

"No, I'm good with numbers," she replied, her hands shaking harder. "We're leaving," she called. "You stay there, and no one has to get hurt."

For a second, silence greeted us. Then the man sighed. "I wish that were true."

Saphira's jaw twitched. "Everly, *run*." She glanced at me, her irises darkening. "*Now*."

I stumbled back a few steps, unsure what to do. Leaving her behind didn't feel right, but she was a *dragon*. If anyone was going to kick this guy's ass, it was *not* me.

The guy ran from behind the red spruce, and my mouth opened to warn her, but no words came out.

She jerked her attention back to him and fired the weapon a few more times, but each bullet missed as he charged toward us.

When he was five feet from her, she aimed the gun

right at the center of his body. At this proximity, I doubted she'd miss. As she pulled the trigger, he spun to the right, away from the car, and lunged at her. He sacked her, and she fell on her back with him right on top of her. He forced the hand holding the gun over her head.

Growling, she clawed at his chest and tried to kick him between the legs.

He shifted his weight, blocking the cheap shot with his thigh, and punched her in the face. Her head jerked, and her eyes rolled into the back of her head.

My throat closed. He'd knocked her out with one blow. Now I was alone with the psycho.

Once he'd pried the gun from her hand, the man rose to his feet. I backed away, not sure what to do. If I ran, I'd be like prey he could hunt, but if I stayed, he'd definitely take me. But how could I leave Saphira after she'd tried to protect me?

"Please don't run," he said. "Then I'll have to chase you...and I will if you make me."

I shook my head, taking a few more steps back. "I don't know what you want from me. I have nothing."

He blew out a breath. "If you don't get on the ATV, I'll be forced to hurt your friend. Is that what you want?"

"No, but I don't want to go with you, either." I gestured to the woods. "Let us go."

"If I could, I would." He charged at me.

I opened my mouth to scream, but he was already there, sticking a needle into my neck. The world tilted as my body went slack, and I fell into his arms.

He whispered, "I've got you."

I wanted to laugh. *He has me*. He was the reason I was drugged, but my tongue grew thick, and my eyes closed, forcing sleep upon me.

Something pounded rhythmically, waking me. My head throbbed, and I touched it, wondering if my pulse was making the noise.

Another round of thumps echoed in random succession...not my pulse.

I opened my eyes and found myself in a room I'd never seen before. The stark off-white walls reminded me of my dorm and hurt my eyes, even though the lights weren't on. I lay on a queen bed, covered by a light blue sheet. A dresser sat in the right corner of the room, next to a window with steel bars over it.

In the opposite corner, an open door revealed a small bathroom with a toilet and a shower.

I sat up quickly and groaned. The room spun from whatever drugs were wearing off.

Drugs.

Bars.

The air sawed through my lungs.

That man had captured me.

Saphira.

She wasn't here with me. I jumped to my feet and lost my balance, falling into the wall.

CHAPTER FIVE

A HARD *BANG* hit the wall above my head, the sound desperate and determined.

It had to be Saphira.

She was alive and here. The room swirled around me, and I placed my hands against the wall to steady myself.

"Saphira?" I croaked. I swallowed to ease the dryness in my throat, but it didn't help.

Silence.

Maybe I'd been imagining things, or she couldn't hear me—which would make sense, because I couldn't hear her. I cleared my throat and winced, but I forced myself to speak louder. She had dragon hearing, after all. "Saphira?" My throat felt as if it were bleeding.

Something thudded against the wall again, but it sounded different...as if her head or body were leaning back on it.

That had to be her. I chose to believe it, even if it was wishful thinking.

I laughed, the sound not unlike a whale's mating call.

My body was functioning at half-capacity from whatever tranquilizer our attacker had used on me.

The pummeling started back up, confirming it was her. If it was our attacker, and if he was that desperate to see me, he'd be waltzing in right about now.

My stomach soured. He couldn't be far away.

Needing all my focus, I used the wall to support myself and took two steps back to sit on the bed. The springs creaked under my weight, and my head pounded harder. This felt worse than what I imagined a hangover would be like, and that was saying something.

I gripped my head with one hand and placed the other on the mattress to steady myself. Something cool pressed into my palm.

I lifted my hand to find my bracelet lying there...broken.

A sharp pain struck my heart, and my breathing turned ragged. This had been my worst fear and one reason I never wore the bracelet. The clasp was broken, and I couldn't fix it, especially here.

I ran a finger over the quote, the engraving scraping my skin.

My chest shook, and I tried to hold in my crying, but a sob broke through, and tears dripped down my cheeks.

The banging on the wall started all over again.

She must be able to hear me. I should have tried to reassure her, but between the heartbreak and my head swirling, I could barely stay upright.

Footsteps sounded, and I jerked my head up and focused on the thick oak door. A square cutout had a metal flap over it like a small access panel in a prison cell. The doorknob jiggled, and I brushed my tears away.

It was him.

Attacker Dragon.

Something slid into the handle, and I held my breath. *Please don't let him come in here.* He'd drugged and kidnapped me. There was no telling what he might do next.

The door opened...and the first thing I noticed was his eyes.

Even after all the horrible stuff he'd done, they intrigued me.

Oh, hell no, Everly, I chastised myself. *You will not develop even the slightest version of Stockholm syndrome. You're not* that *desperate for an emotional bond. You've been fine on your own for the past six years.*

He scanned me as he entered the room and shut the door behind him with a bare foot. His nose wrinkled. He carried a plate with a sandwich on it and a glass of water, both of which he held out to me, muscles bulging under his black cotton shirt. "Here. Eat this so you stop crying."

My bottom lip quivered, but I straightened my shoulders. I refused to look weak, even though we both knew he had all the control. I'd pretend to have my dignity—like I'd done for a long while now. "Eating won't make me feel better," I rasped. "You were outside Dragon Alley the other night. I *saw* you."

"Yes. I have to keep an eye on my enemies, and fortunately, I was there—because it led me to you." He walked to a small table underneath the window and set down the plate, then turned his back to me for a moment, not worried about me running away.

"Did you hear me? I don't want it." I clutched the bracelet and wished the sluggishness would go away. I was acting childish, but I couldn't help it.

"Oh, believe me, I can *hear* you." He spun around and

sneered. "I hear you and *your friend* everywhere in this damn cabin. If you two would just be quiet, we could all get some rest."

Thank good. It *was* her. I sniffled, trying to pull myself together. A snotty nose wouldn't help matters. "I *just* woke up, so clearly, I'm not the issue."

"You weren't until you started bawling like a toddler." He gestured to the food. "So eat up, and stop acting so emotional."

"Excuse *me*." I attempted to stand, but the wood floor seemed to move, and I landed back on my butt. The disorientation from whatever barbiturate he'd given me was awful. If he was uncomfortable with noise, I'd make his life hell, offering him the same courtesy he'd afforded me. "Let's see. You're a fucking dragon. You kidnapped me by flying me away in a car. Then you *drugged* me. Let me tell you: death feels pretty damn imminent. And you broke the last meaningful thing my mother gave me before she died, so yeah, *I'm* being *emotional*?" The words raked against my raw throat, but that pain was nothing compared to the trauma he was putting me through. "I'd say that makes you criminally insensitive."

A loud flurry of thumps sounded again.

The attacker winced but kept his focus on me. His jaw twitched. "I don't care if you think you're being overly emotional. You've made me out to be a bad guy. I haven't hurt you—"

"Yeah, right. You merely *drugged* me and knocked Saphira out." I should keep my mouth shut. I knew the side effects of tranquilizers, and I was experiencing at least three: impaired judgment, mood swings, and anger. "Yet you come in here and bring me a sandwich and water like you care."

He snorted, his damn face sexy even with a scowl. "Because I'm clearly an insensitive bastard."

I frowned. How could I argue with that? And agreeing with him didn't make it satisfying. This was *not* how this conversation was supposed to go. "Uh...*yeah*." I threw out a hand...and toppled over.

Saphira slammed into the wall, and it vibrated from her assault. I didn't understand how she hadn't broken through.

In fact, I needed to get off this bed before she did break through so I wouldn't be in her way.

When I stood, the floor didn't shift under my feet. I glanced at our attacker, who didn't seem concerned about her at all.

He rolled his eyes. "I haven't touched her."

Of course *he* could hear her. I was the lone wolf—no, *human* here and didn't have the equivalent of Spidey-senses for dragons.

"If you haven't touched me, then how did I get into this bed?" I lifted a brow and sidestepped, trying to regain my balance. Maybe I should eat. I didn't like feeling this way.

His breathing turned ragged. "Would you rather I'd left you unconscious outside for a hungry animal to find?"

No, he didn't get to act like a hero. "If you hadn't drugged me, that wouldn't *have been* a problem!"

Saphira redoubled her attack on the wall.

"It doesn't matter why you're here. It only matters that you *are*." He rolled his shoulders, looking rugged and strong. "Eat the sandwich or don't. I don't give a fuck." He shrugged as if he couldn't care less. "I'm providing you with what you need to survive. It's up to you to care enough to do it."

My lungs wheezed at the truth he'd laid out. He could let us slowly starve and fade away, but instead, he'd brought food. Squeezing the bracelet tightly in my hands, I used it to anchor myself. I was making the situation more volatile. I needed something, *anything* on which to focus this anger and frustration.

Instead of answering, I breathed through my nose to calm the raging storm inside me. My body was shaking, and I hated it. When I got super upset, I always looked scared or worse. I didn't want to give our attacker more of an ego boost because he didn't need any help in that department.

He held out his hand. "Give me your bracelet."

I shook my head and clutched the hand holding the bracelet to my chest. He'd already broken it; there was no way I was handing it over.

His pupils slitted, hinting at the dragon within.

My knees locked, and I swayed again. The hair on the nape of my neck lifted. The last thing I wanted was to be stuck in a room alone with a freaking dragon. For some reason, though, he didn't seem as scary in human form, but the beast was in there somewhere.

He moved closer and loomed over me. He was almost two feet taller than me, and I had to tilt my head back to stare at his face and not his chest. His mouth tightened, and his minty-amber scent, mixed with a hint of sulfur, swirled around me. "I didn't ask, *human*."

He was trying to intimidate me, and I hated that it was working. My heart raced so quickly that my chest ached, and I swallowed back a scream. A tiny squeak escaped.

Saphira quit banging, and a loud *thud* echoed in this room as if she'd run full speed into the wall.

I winced. The sound was bad enough on this side. I could only imagine how hard she'd hit her side of the wall.

"I can't part with it," I whispered, emotion thick in my voice. The thought of him taking it from me had me damn near falling to pieces.

He pulled the hand holding the bracelet away from my chest. His touch was uncomfortably hot, as if he'd just stepped out of a steaming shower. With his other hand, he dug his fingers into the flesh between my fingertips and my palm, loosening my grip on the bracelet.

"No!" I shouted, and yanked backward, slamming into the wall across from the window and close to the door. "Please. Don't take it." I hated begging, but that was all I had to work with. He couldn't take the last meaningful thing I possessed.

A very muffled scream came from the other side of the wall, and our attacker rolled his eyes. He yelled, "You know you can't get through that. The entire room is sealed with Wolfram Dwiin." And he pried the bracelet from my hands.

Heat ran through my blood as my anger took root. I didn't care if he was a dragon—that wasn't his to take. I threw myself against his chest and pounded my hands against him. I channeled strength from the rage inside me. It felt as if I were hitting steel, but I didn't let that deter me.

"Stop!" he bellowed.

That only encouraged me. Maybe I was stronger than I realized? For a moment, I allowed myself to believe the illusion. I thrashed against him and groaned in complete frustration. My hands ached, but I had to believe it was because I was making the impact I desperately needed.

"Dear gods," he snarled. He grabbed me by my shoulders and lifted me off the floor. My feet dangled, giving me another opportunity to attack him. I kicked and grabbed his muscular chest, digging my fingernails into his skin.

I might as well have been kicking a damn rock. My toes ached from the impact, and my fingernails hadn't made as much as a dent in his skin. He tossed me onto the bed, and my head jerked back, causing the walls to spin once again.

"I said *stop*." His voice rang with power. "Don't make me hurt you."

I laughed manically, the last of my sanity leaving me. "You already have. You're taking away *everything*."

"You're about to see what pain feels like," he snarled.

Saphira's barrage on the wall kept time with my pulse pounding in my ears. As I stared at my attacker, I realized he meant every word. He would hurt me if I didn't stop, so I wrapped my arms around my legs and pulled them against my chest. I rocked myself, trying to focus on any good memories, but they all slid away like my freedom.

He was silent for a moment, and then he huffed. "Look, if I put you in the same room as your *friend*, will that calm the two of you down?"

I went still. I hadn't expected that after he'd threatened to hurt me. Being with her would be more comforting. I nodded, afraid if I said the words, my voice would break.

Lines creased his forehead, and he ran a hand down his face. "I'm not doing it for you. It's for me. I need sleep. *Good* sleep. And that can't be achieved with *you* crying and *her* trying to get out of that room, even though it's impossible." He moved his hair, flipping it out of his eyes. "I'll put you together if you promise to calm down."

I'd rather have my bracelet, but that wouldn't happen. "Fine."

He pointed at the door. "Come on. You're moving in there with her, not the other way around."

I jumped to my feet, not wanting to give him time to change his mind. I hurried to the door and threw it open.

For some reason, I hadn't expected to step into a hallway. I glanced left and noted another bedroom that looked similar to the room I'd been in. The hallway stretched from that room to the other end of the house, but I couldn't make out anything more.

Dammit, I'd been hoping to get a sense of the layout.

"You know which direction her room is in," the man growled behind me. "*Move*."

He must have realized what I was trying to do. He did seem intelligent.

I turned right and hurried to the last door on that side. I grabbed the doorknob and turned, but it was locked.

"Did you really think it'd be open?" he asked sarcastically. He moved beside me, pulled a key out of his pocket, then slipped it into the lock.

"One wrong move, and this is over," he said and lifted a brow at me. Then he addressed the door, "When I open this, nothing had better happen."

After a second, I heard someone move away on the other side.

She must have been waiting for an opportunity to escape. Why hadn't I thought of that? I was so desperate to get to her that I hadn't considered running.

He opened the door and pushed me inside so fast that I tripped over my own feet.

CHAPTER SIX

BEFORE I COULD HIT the floor, Saphira caught me under my arms. The room swirled again, though not as quickly. The drugs were wearing off.

The door slammed as she growled, "What the hell was that? I wasn't trying anything."

"I wasn't going to wait to see." He exhaled on the other side of the door. "She was already snooping while just moving rooms, and I don't trust either of you."

She steadied me on my feet, and I surveyed the room. Dark metal covered the entire space from the floor to the ceiling. The bars over the window were the same as mine, but the door was covered with the same metal as well. "What *is* that?"

Her room was similar to mine with the bed against the outside wall, a window to the left, and a small dresser in the right corner. A tiny bathroom backed to the one in my room, hers in the far left corner. Like the bedroom, the bathroom was covered with metal, and I wondered how the hell he expected her to take a shower on a wet metal surface.

Shit. I was already thinking that we would be here long enough to need to bathe. My feet were caked in dirt from running barefoot in the woods.

"Your room isn't covered in Wolfram Dwiin?" She reached out and touched the wall.

"If that's what you're calling this metal, no." I'd never heard of it before, which was peculiar. I'd taken a ton of chemistry classes for premed. "It looks like aluminum foil." I slid a foot against the floor and realized the metal wasn't as smooth as it appeared. It was a little grainy to the touch. "Except it's not smooth."

Interesting.

I studied the wall to see what made it feel like sandpaper.

She snorted but somehow still seemed elegant. When I snorted, I was fairly certain I resembled a pig.

"This is most definitely *not* aluminum foil." She flicked her wrist. "This is dragon tungsten. It's the strongest metal in the world, forged by dragon fire."

Tungsten I'd heard of, especially with all the commercials about wedding bands.

"Any dragon can make it?" I laid my hand on top of it and pressed. It felt like one of those pin art boards I'd played with as a kid. It didn't hurt, but it wasn't comfortable.

"Only the strongest of our kind can." Saphira's tone hardened. "Which means our captor has a powerful friend."

"Why couldn't it be him?" I asked as I turned my head toward her.

She sighed and moved to her queen-sized bed, also with blue sheets. She plopped down on the mattress and touched the left side of her head, where our attacker had hit her. "The strongest of our kind are the royal line, and neither Drake nor his father would *do* this."

I swallowed hard. My curiosity and the drugs had dulled my anxiety, but now my shoulders tensed. "What do you mean, *royal* line?"

She dropped her hand. "What *did* Drake tell you?"

"That he wanted someone who wasn't after his money to be his wife and have his heirs." My skin crawled, but I held my body still. Drake had trusted her to come get me, suggesting they were friends. That relationship didn't add up. She seemed like a nice, caring person. I doubted Drake would've protected me the way she had.

She stared at me and opened her mouth, exhaling. Placing her hands on her lap, she shook her head. "That's surprising. Prince Drake is never one to hold back about his status or his wealth."

"Then maybe he planned this." Narcissists did anything for attention and empathy. They strove for control and power, and during the handful of times I'd seen Drake, I could tell those were his priorities. "This is a good way to make him out to be a martyr."

"Please." She waved a hand. "He's all about power. Your kidnapping will make him appear weak in the eyes of our people. Believe me, this is *not* his doing, and the king wouldn't do anything to upset his son. Maybe this guy found some Wolfram Dwiin that was made a long time ago. I thought it was all locked up somewhere central, but there could be more."

When she put it that way, I understood. I could see that about Drake. "I'm assuming Drake's award-winning personality is why we're in this mess. Has he pissed off enough of his subjects, or is the *prince* title a formality with no real meaning?"

"Wow, you sure jumped in without knowing the facts." She pursed her lips. "You seem like a 'think things through' type of girl, not one who leaps without knowing what she's getting into."

"Oh, believe me, I am." I sat beside her on the bed and clutched one of the pillows in my lap. "I didn't realize 'What species are you?' was a legitimate question. You all *look* human. How was I supposed to know there was a dragon hidden inside him?" I still didn't understand how that was possible. I squinted as I stared into her eyes, trying to see a hint of the creature within her.

She laughed, her worry fading as her face smoothed into a genuine smile. "That's fair. We hide our existence from humans. And there isn't a dragon inside us. It's more like the soul of a dragon courses through us."

My heart fluttered as my body overheated. Somehow, that explanation freaked me out more. The thought of an animal soul being inside them made them sound unstable.

"Do you need to use the bathroom?" Saphira bit her bottom lip and scooted to the edge of the bed.

Here I was, feeling unsettled, and she was the one inching away from me. "No. Why?"

"You're flushed, and you look sick. Are you going to puke, or is it about to come out the *other* end?" Her face wrinkled as if she smelled something bad. "Even though I'm a dragon, I have a weak stomach when it comes to *that*."

I covered my face with my hands. There was no telling what my expression had looked like for her mind to go there. "No, I'm not going to puke or...poop." Wow.

That last part had been way too hard to say when I wanted to become a doctor. "But if an animal's soul is loose in you...doesn't that make you, like, constantly at odds?"

Her eyes widened. "Oh, that's what's wrong with you? You think I could go all dragony at any second?"

Well, yeah. "That's not an unreasonable assumption."

"And this is why we don't tell humans." Saphira rubbed her temples. "Which is probably why Drake didn't tell you. Though I bet he wanted to tell you he's a prince. He brings it up in every conversation, despite each of us being well aware."

"At least it makes more sense that he was so focused on my appearance. He said that with his dominant features and my symmetry and figure, his heirs would be appealing." Though I wasn't sure it made his comments *that* much better. He'd still treated me as less than a person, but perhaps, since I wasn't a dragon, he naturally viewed me that way.

She rolled her eyes but readjusted herself on the mattress, comforted that I wouldn't hurl on her. "That does sound like Drake. He's a little intense."

That was an understatement. "Can you explain the dragon thing?"

"Oh, yeah." She stood and paced the small area between the bed and the wall. "It's not like our animal is constantly trying to take over or battle for control. Our dragon is deep inside us, and for the most part, it's content. Magic pumps through our blood, and when we call forth the dragon to either fly or fight, our shift is a natural transformation."

I leaned forward, hanging on to her every word.

Though I was listening, I still had to be missing things. However, I took away the key idea that was relevant to me —they called forth the dragon, not the other way around. "Does it ever take over?"

When she stopped in her tracks and frowned, my entire body froze.

"If we don't shift often enough, yes. Our dragon can get anxious and try to take control." She pushed her long curly hair behind her shoulders. "Our dragon side is as much a part of us as our human side. We're neither human nor dragon but shifter. All shifters have similar struggles."

The information crashed over me like a wave pulling me under. "How often do you need to shift? And there are other types of shifters out there?" All my life, I'd studied as much about the world as possible, but now I wondered if I actually knew anything.

"There are also wolf shifters and bear shifters." She placed her hands behind her back. "But not any other kind that I know of."

At least there was that...I guessed. Right now, I needed to learn most about my immediate threat—dragons. "You didn't answer my question about how often you need to shift." Was she avoiding telling me? My palms were sweaty, and I wiped them on my black shorts.

"Once a week at minimum," she whispered. "But I shifted three days ago, and we'll find a way out before then."

A lump formed in my throat. We had four days until her dragon took control, and since this room wasn't big enough to hold her in that form, I wasn't sure what that would look like. One thing I was fairly confident about was that if I didn't find a way out of this room before she had to shift, I would likely get crushed and die. "What if we *don't* and I'm in here with you? I'll be squashed."

"I can't shift in this metal prison. If we stay here that long, I'll lose my mind as my dragon tries to take over but can't." She smiled sadly as if she was trying to reassure me.

That didn't help *at all.* "Uh…so I'd be stuck in here with a woman whose dragon soul is trying to take control and failing. That doesn't sound much safer."

She placed her hands on my shoulders and stared into my eyes as she vowed, "We'll find a way out of here before then."

I smiled. She was reassuring me the same way Mom would have. It was the most kindness anyone had shown me in a long time, and I didn't want to dismiss it. "Let's take it day by day."

"That's all we can do." She stood up and winced as she clutched her head.

She might have a concussion from getting knocked out. The best thing she could do was lie down and rest.

"First, let's get some sleep." I slid off the bed and landed on my knees. "We both need it if we're going to find a way out of here."

Exhaling, she nodded. "That's a good idea." She stared at me. "Why are you on the ground? That metal will *not* be comfortable to sleep on."

Though it was grainy, I was tired enough that I was certain I could fall asleep. "It'll be fine."

"We just got kidnapped together." She pointed to the side of the bed by the window. "You take that side, and I'll sleep here."

My heart expanded, tightening my chest. She was taking the side of the bed closest to the door. "Uh...thanks. Let me wash my feet before I crawl into bed." I'd rather take a shower, but I had no clean clothes to change into. Another issue for tomorrow.

She nodded, and I rushed into the bathroom. The metal-coated shower was just big enough for one person to stand in, and I almost cried when I turned on the water and it ran. The toilet wasn't metal, but the sink was covered with it.

Our kidnapper must have thought that we wouldn't risk trying to escape via the toilet. He wasn't wrong.

There was a bar of soap on the sink and in the shower, along with bottles of shampoo and conditioner, which I found odd. He'd kidnapped us but made sure we had toiletries. Not wanting to overthink it, I washed my feet quickly and searched for a towel. The only one I could find was the hand towel by the sink, but that would have to work.

Once I got clean and used the toilet, I headed back into the room. Saphira was already lying on the bed with her eyes closed. The sun was just setting, but it wasn't like we had much to do, so I slid in beside her and was out within seconds.

SOMETHING CLICKED, stirring me from sleep. Was my roommate waking up to go to class?

When the mattress moved, reality crashed over me. I wasn't at the university. I'd been kidnapped, and there was no telling where we were.

A low snarl came from Saphira, and I opened my

eyes, finding myself staring at the window. I sat up just as the door opened.

Our attacker strolled in and shut the door, blocking it so Saphira and I couldn't go around him. He held two cups of coffee. Steam drifted from the tops, and I leaned toward him.

After a night of not drinking anything, I needed something for my throat.

His hair was wet from a shower, and his white shirt clung to his skin, emphasizing each muscle. His dark jeans molded to his legs, and the sad truth was, if I'd met him outside of this horrible situation, he would have interested me.

He held out one cup to Saphira and the other to me. "I thought you two might want some coffee while I make breakfast," he rasped.

The last thing I wanted to do was accept a cup of coffee from him, but my pride wasn't stronger than my need for caffeine and something to drink. I rolled across the bed, and when I tried to stand, I fell hard onto the floor and onto Saphira's foot.

Okay, maybe all the drugs weren't out of my system.

Saphira grunted and yanked her foot out from under me, and my face burned as I got up.

Now that my pride had completely vanished, I was certain there was no salvaging it.

He stretched the cup of coffee toward me and chuckled. "You clearly need this."

A few choice responses popped into my head, but I swallowed them down. I might not trust him, but if I didn't drink or eat something, I wouldn't last very long.

Saphira must have had the same thought because she

grabbed her cup at the same time I did, our attacker watching our every move.

There it was. He was still in attack mode, ready to spring into action.

As I put the cup to my lips, our attacker said, "Oh, and I've got something for you."

He reached into his pocket, and I tensed.

CHAPTER SEVEN

I HAD no clue what to do. He'd brought coffee, which seemed too good to be true. He must be using the caffeine to distract us from whatever was in his pocket.

Even if I had taken a self-defense class, it wouldn't have helped me. This guy was a *fucking dragon*. I was confident that even if I could remember the moves I'd learned, they wouldn't work against him.

Saphira paused with the coffee cup half an inch from her lips.

I wasn't the only wary one.

He struggled to remove whatever was in his pocket, putting me more on edge. My heart raced, and my body tensed. I hated feeling helpless.

"Finally," he grumbled as he withdrew his hand.

A scream lodged in the back of my throat as Saphira thrust her coffee at me, and I took it. A little bit of the hot liquid splashed over the rim onto my hand, but getting burned was the least of my worries.

She stepped in front of me...just as he removed my bracelet from his pocket.

His brows furrowed as he glanced at Saphira and me. He lifted the bracelet by the newly fixed clasp and said, "What the *hell* is your problem?"

"What in the world?" Saphira gestured at the jewelry. "You brought us a *gift*?"

I pivoted around Saphira and shoved both mugs of coffee into her hands. I blinked as my shaky hand reached out to snatch the jewelry from him, but I stopped short. This could be a trick. "That's *my* bracelet. He broke it yesterday and took it from me." He had to be playing some kind of demented game.

"I...fixed it." He held out the bracelet to me. "I thought you'd be happy."

Kidnappers didn't do things out of kindness, and I wasn't stupid. We'd seen his face.

Unbridled rage soared through me. Now that it'd been released, the flames were hotter and brighter. "I'd be happier if you hadn't *kidnapped* us. Then you wouldn't have needed to fix it in the first place!"

His jaw twitched, and his pupils slitted. The flames cooled as fear rooted inside me. If we were going to die, I didn't want to make it happen earlier than he planned.

"No wonder Drake picked you." Our kidnapper scowled. "You're as entitled as *he* is."

The words cut worse than anything physical he could've done. I despised Drake, especially since he'd locked me into marriage without telling me what I'd become a part of. "I'm not entitled. Did you really expect a *thank you*?" I swallowed, trying to keep my voice even.

"What are you trying to accomplish?" Saphira squinted at him. "I'm not buying this whole 'nice guy' act."

He laughed bitterly. "Oh, and you're such a *nice* girl. *She* didn't even know dragons existed until the attack."

I placed my hands on my hips. "How did you know that?"

"The fear you displayed yesterday and now," he answered smugly. "You don't even want to reach out to take back the bracelet that means so much to you."

I hated that he'd guessed that. I'd worked hard since Mom had died to hide my emotions behind a perfect fake smile. Current circumstances had ruined that completely, and I was afraid I'd never be able to pretend again. A chill ran down my spine.

Was this my life now—a lifetime as his or Drake's servant, doing whatever they desired?

"Fine. You want her to have her *fixed* bracelet," Saphira snapped, and handed me back my coffee. She reached out and took the bracelet from him. "There. Consider it done. You're obviously such a *nice guy* and wanted to take care of us." She lifted the bracelet and the coffee cup, emphasizing her point.

His neck corded, and his hand blurred as he clasped Saphira's cup. "Treating you like prisoners will make this easier for *me*." He pulled on the cup, and the liquid spilled.

I stumbled back a few steps, not wanting to be caught near these two as they fought each other. They could land on me and squash me like a bug. I gulped in a breath, trying to remain quiet.

"Wait!" Saphira exclaimed and lowered her lips to the rim of the cup.

What in the world was she doing?

"Prisoners don't get to make demands," he snarled and jerked the cup again.

Saphira had already placed her lips on the cup, and her whole body moved with it. She raised the hand with the bracelet and pressed it against his chest for balance.

She tipped the mug, taking a large sip before he pushed her off him. He frowned as his attention flicked between the mug and her. He tipped the mug up and drained the rest of the liquid. His attention then homed in on me, and he swiped my mug and drank it all, too.

The coffee had been super hot, more so than I was used to. The liquid had scalded my hand, so I had no idea how he'd drained two full mugs that quickly. Then I realized he was a fire-breathing dragon. That liquid was probably like a cool drink of water to him.

That all-too-familiar trickle of fear clawed in my chest, weakening my knees. I didn't regret my decision to take Eva's place, but damn, I wished I weren't here.

"You *bastard*," Saphira growled.

Our attacker's face hardened as he glared down his nose at her. He sneered, "I tried to be nice, but you complained, so we're back to square one. Watch your tone, or you won't get any breakfast. I know the human can last longer than *you* can without food. Behave, or I won't even provide the essentials."

Her irises flashed with anger, and smoke trickled from her nostrils.

I froze. This further proved how little I knew about dragons.

"What do you want from us?" I whispered. "I don't know you."

The angry lines on his face smoothed. "It isn't you that I'm after. You're just a means to an end."

Once again, I was missing something. "What could capturing me accomplish?"

Saphira pressed a hand to her stomach. "He wants something from the *prince*."

It took a second for me to understand. Even though Drake had entitlement issues, I didn't yet correlate that with "prince." In my mind kings, queens, and princes should do everything they could for their people and be selfless, hardworking, and caring. Three qualities I was confident Drake lacked. "I hate to break it to you, but I don't mean a damn thing to him. I'm replaceable."

Our kidnapper snorted. "Did you think it was smart to agree to belong to a man you don't know? Were you that hard up for money or attention? Because you're in over your head with no fucking clue what's going on."

His sinister tone caused me to step closer to Saphira. Though she was a dragon, I felt safe with her.

"And now you're looking for safety with someone who also doesn't have your best interest at heart." He gave an exaggerated eye roll. "Maybe you should work on your instincts before they get you killed."

Despite his cruelty, there was truth behind each word. Either that, or he was an amazing manipulator, but something about him made me *want* to trust him.

Oh, hell. He was right. My instincts were messed up.

Saphira edged in front of me and pointed a finger at him. "I don't know who you think you are or what you know about me, but you're wrong. Drake may be my prince, but I think for myself. I don't need a *man* telling me what to do."

"So you have nothing to hide?" The corners of his eyes tightened as he watched her. "Nothing you would rather she not know?"

"Of course not." Saphira glanced at me and back at

him. "Drake asked me to pick her up because the king needed to meet with him. I obliged. That's all."

He gestured at me. "You think she knows what she signed up for? She didn't even know he was a dragon."

She flinched.

My skin prickled, and I stepped away from Saphira. He was trying to turn us against each other, but I sensed there *was* something more I didn't know.

My vision dotted as I grew short of breath. "What else is there?" My voice squeaked.

"Tell her," our kidnapper taunted.

She turned to me, her cheeks turning a faint pink. "I truly thought you were aware of everything."

"All I knew was that I agreed to marry a *man*." I took a few steps back, wanting to get away from both of them. "Now there are dragons, and there's something else I don't know."

Saphira cringed, and our kidnapper laughed humorlessly.

I gasped, trying to catch my breath. The room suddenly seemed devoid of oxygen.

"Is *that* what you think he wants you for?" the kidnapper asked. "As a wife?"

My mind replayed our conversation at the bar. "He said he needed someone to be his, someone he could trust not to be after his money and to provide heirs. What else—"

"Your future is as his *breeder*," the kidnapper spat. "He'll marry another dragon while you're kept somewhere in the house, at his beck and call."

The world tilted, and I clutched the footboard of the bed for balance. "No." I locked eyes with Saphira and croaked, "Tell me that's not true."

She averted her gaze to the floor. "I..." She trailed off, unsure what to say.

My chin trembled. After she'd gone all out to protect me, I'd trusted her, thinking she was a good person. Now I knew the *real* reason. "Why? Why does he need *me* if he'll have a dragon as his queen?"

"Because dragons have a hard time reproducing, and our numbers are dwindling," Saphira answered in a rush. She hung her head. "We're trying to find a quicker way to reproduce."

"Trying?" This kept getting worse. "Like...this hasn't been done before?" My heart jumped into my throat. I hadn't considered carrying a *dragon baby* inside me. How would that even work?

She picked at her fingers, not answering.

My kidnapper had no problem filling me in. "You'll be one of the first humans they try this with. There's no telling if it'll work or if you'll survive."

No wonder Drake had wanted someone without strong familial ties. I could die, and it would be years before anyone asked about me...if they ever did.

Tears burned my eyes. I'd thought I'd felt worthless before, but boy, had I been wrong. *This* was the epitome of worthlessness. "And you knew?" I glanced at Saphira. I needed to hear her say it.

"Everly, until we spoke today, I thought *you* knew." Saphira twirled a piece of her hair around her finger. "I swear. I know Drake is self-absorbed and has borderline ethics, but I didn't realize he was this far gone. I didn't know how to tell you or if I should."

She could justify it all she wanted. At the end of the day, I was a human, so I didn't count. I was a means to an end, even if it resulted in my death.

I laughed. I hated to admit it, but the kidnapper had a point. "I didn't know about the supernatural world, so even if I had known about the breeding part, I wouldn't have known I might *die*."

She opened her mouth and closed it.

Good. At least she wouldn't talk out of her ass anymore.

I straightened my shoulders. "Take me back to my cell."

"What?" Her mouth dropped open. "No! We need to stay together."

I laughed again, the sound making my stomach roil. "Why? To protect me so I can die a brutal death when a dragon baby rips its way out of my body? I'd rather take my chances with *him*." I pointed at our kidnapper.

Something like sadness reflected in our kidnapper's eyes, but it had to be a figment of my imagination. I was done trusting anyone...especially *dragons*.

"I'll take you back to your room." He turned and grasped the door handle.

Saphira grabbed my arm. "Everly, don't go. I get it, I messed up. But when I came to collect you, I seriously thought you knew everything. *I'm sorry*. Please stay here with me."

Something tugged at my heart, but I pushed it away. I wouldn't keep making foolish decisions. "I need space."

I jerked my arm, expecting her to hold tight. She could make me stay if she wanted to, but she released me.

"Please. Stay," she begged again.

"You heard her." The kidnapper opened the door and plucked the bracelet from her hand. "She wants to go back to her room, and I don't blame her. All you people are out for yourselves."

He spoke as if he had experience.

Once I walked out the door, he shut it and locked it behind me, and panic set in. He had me alone again without Saphira for protection.

I'd let him play me, and now I wondered what he'd do.

CHAPTER EIGHT

I REGRETTED LEAVING SAPHIRA, but I couldn't stay with her, either. I no longer trusted her. The kidnapper had made her allegiance to Drake clear.

Hurt ripped through me, and I hated that I'd let my guard down. I guessed that was what happened when you were thrown into a chaotic situation with people you didn't know. Saphira and I had forged a bond of captives, but I would be a captive at Drake's place as well. She'd be free.

This was why I didn't let anyone close. I always got hurt.

Our kidnapper slid around me and slipped the key into the lock of my room. He opened it and pointed inside. "No funny business."

I didn't have it in me. The sting of betrayal was fresh, and I blinked several times to hold back tears.

I stepped back into the room and inhaled deeply. I scanned the space and realized the sandwich he'd left me yesterday was gone.

He must have cleaned up behind me.

Holding both mugs in one hand, he came in and shut the door.

I'd expected him to lock me in and leave, but nope. There he stood.

His features softened, taking away the dangerous edge. I needed it back because my stomach started fluttering without it. There was no denying that he was sexy.

I sat on the mattress and ran my hands over the sheets, the void of loneliness growing colder inside me.

He strolled over and held out his hand, letting the bracelet dangle. "Here. Take this."

Unable to fight the urge, I obliged. Part of me expected him to yank it away and make fun of me, but when warm metal touched my fingers, he released it. His hand had heated it up.

I swallowed hard, the years of manners Mom had ingrained in me coming forward. "Thank you."

His brows furrowed. "That's the last thing you should say."

"Huh?" My brain was struggling to keep up. My thoughts kept flitting back to Drake and Saphira instead of focusing on our conversation.

"You just thanked me." He shook his head, his long bangs blocking part of his eyes. "You shouldn't. Fixing your bracelet is the least I could do."

If I hadn't known any better, I could've sworn I was talking to a different man. Yet I was still a prisoner locked in a bedroom, so this had to be a game. "I don't know what you're trying to accomplish, but you can quit being nice. Yes, you called Saphira out for what she's part of, but that doesn't make us *friends*. I'm still your *captive*...unless I'm not? In which case, I'd like to get the *hell* out of here."

"I can't let you go. I'm sorry." He bit his bottom lip

and frowned. "I wish I could, but there's a reason for all of this."

I'd heard the same refrain over and over again since Mom's death. Reasons always abounded, and they always benefited someone else. I was expendable...a means to someone else's ends. "Don't. I get it. There's something you want that's more important than me."

"Look, I don't know you, but you have a jaded view of yourself. You're beautiful and strong and—"

"Stop." Was this guy for real? He must have thought I was so hard up that throwing a few flattering words at me would make me stay here willingly. "Don't pretend to be a nice guy. Just stay the asshole we both know you are."

I was usually good at biting my tongue and playing whatever role my audience wanted, but I was so damn tired. This whole "taking my sister's place to become a dragon prince's mistress and bear his heir that could possibly kill me at any time" development had broken me. That didn't take into account getting kidnapped. Every time I thought things couldn't get worse, something out there proved me wrong, not that I believed in a higher power or anything.

He nodded. "I can do that." He opened the door and glanced back at me. "But I am sorry. You don't deserve this."

Gritting my teeth, I readied myself to yell at him to get out, but he was already closing the door. I flopped onto my bed and stared at the ceiling, rubbing my thumb around the inscription on my bracelet and trying not to think about what would happen to me.

The day crawled by, and my boredom reached the point where I'd stand at the window and try to count all the raindrops that fell from the sky. The light dimmed as the sun set behind the leaden clouds. Dragon Guy had brought me some basil chicken and pasta for dinner, and I was now eating at the table, still staring at the raindrops.

I cut off a piece of chicken with the butter knife and the fork he'd provided and continued my impossible task. I was up to one hundred thousand, and I knew, without a doubt, that wasn't even one-millionth of what had fallen.

At least the room was dry and warm. He could have stuck us in a basement or something not even half this nice.

A door somewhere in the house slammed, and I held my breath, listening. Could he have possibly gone? I hadn't heard that noise before. But he hadn't left the house since Saphira and I had arrived, so that would be a first and most likely wishful thinking.

Placing my fork and knife on the edge of the plate, I leaned forward. My forehead hit the cool metal bars, blocking me from seeing out of the corner of the window, where I assumed a road was, since I could see trees to the left.

An engine rumbled, and I took a step back just as a large, white, beat-up pickup truck rushed by. The silhouette of the person inside was huge, confirming it was our kidnapper.

Blood buzzing, I pressed my face to the window again, watching the taillights shrink and disappear from sight.

He'd actually left and taken a truck and not the ATV, and I hoped that meant he was driving somewhere far away.

This might be my only chance to get out of here and call for help. I spun on my heels and ran for the door. I clutched the doorknob in my hands and turned, praying it opened.

The knob didn't budge.

Dammit. That would've made this whole thing go a lot more smoothly, but that also would have meant that my kidnapper was not intelligent. Unfortunately, that wasn't the case.

I'd just have to be smarter.

I faced the room, pressing my back against the wooden door. I scanned the area for another way out, and my gaze stopped on the end table.

That was it. I would smash my way out.

I placed my plate of food on the floor and grabbed the thin wooden legs of the lightweight table before hurrying back to the door. I grunted as I swung the table against the door with all the force I had. The *bang* was loud, but nothing much happened. The only damage was a small dent on the door and a much larger ding on the edge of the table.

"You've got to be *kidding* me," I muttered. Frustration fueled me, and I lifted the table over my head and slammed it into the same spot.

Something *cracked*, and my heart picked up its pace. It was about damn time something good happened to me, but when I lowered the end table, the thick wooden section on top dropped to the floor with a heavy *thud*.

And the door didn't look much worse than it had moments ago.

Of course he'd pick a sturdy door for this room. That wasn't surprising, considering Saphira's room had all that aluminum foil inside to keep her locked in. This guy had thought everything through.

Something banged against the wall separating Saphira and me. She must have been worried.

I pulled at the ends of my hair, feeling crazy. I wished I could communicate with Saphira somehow. If I'd had her hearing, I was certain we could have, but with my human ears, I might as well be alone.

Unsure what to try next, I dropped the wooden legs and hurried to the bathroom. Maybe there was a way out through there.

I turned on the lights and studied the tiny room. There was a small tub, a toilet, and a sink all crammed together. The room was windowless.

My heart pounded so hard that my ears rang. The sink was a pedestal style, so the wall was exposed on the sides underneath, between the wall and the toilet. Maybe I could knock that out.

I kicked at the drywall, determined to break a hole through it.

It was like hitting a pole.

Right. Dammit, Saphira's bathroom was on the other side and covered in that special metal. If a dragon couldn't get through it, there was no way *I* could. I was only wasting time and energy.

There had to be another way.

I rushed back into the bedroom, my attention locked on the bars over the window. I could try breaking those.

I picked up the two broken-off table legs and circled back to the window. Swinging them as hard as I could, I pounded the middle of the five bars over and over, using all the force I could to crack the metal. With every strike, wood splintered from the legs.

I continued to push, hoping like hell *something* would give.

One leg broke in half, the loose part flying backward and hitting me in the forehead.

Pain exploded from the impact, and I damn near fell over. I sidestepped and caught my balance as something warm ran down my face. Tears welled in my eyes as I tossed the wooden legs on the bed and rushed back into the bathroom to take care of my injury. If I didn't get the wound to clot, I would be in worse shape.

Another round of banging came from the wall, but I ignored it as I snatched some toilet paper and pressed the material to my head. That should keep the gash from getting worse, even if it wasn't the most sanitary treatment. That was an issue for later.

My head throbbed, and I couldn't believe I'd been so foolish. I was so intent on getting *out* that I wasn't using my brain. There was no telling how long he'd be gone, so I had to think critically instead of repeatedly injuring myself.

Stepping back into the room, I took deep breaths to calm my flight instincts and allow the adrenaline to clear my head. I rolled my shoulders, and my gaze landed back on the door.

Breath catching, I developed a different plan.

The hinges. That was my best bet.

But I didn't have a screwdriver or hammer, so how could I get this to work?

I growled and clenched my free hand. Every damn time I got close to thinking of a solution, the plan fell through. It'd be nice for *something* to work while I had the chance.

My attention went back to my dinner plate. The only

good thing about being here so far had been the delicious food. I was wondering how my kidnapper had learned to cook so well when light reflected off the knife.

Body tensing, I feared I might cry tears of relief.

Still clutching the paper to my cut, I stumbled to the butter knife and fell on my knees. That stupid table leg had hit me hard enough that it was messing with my balance. I had to get out of here.

I grasped the knife and slowly marched to the door. Head spinning, I decided to start with the top hinge.

The hinge was new and unpainted, which was what I'd expected. Our kidnapper had gone to great lengths to set this place up to contain us, which meant he'd bought new stuff. The top of the hinge was capped and styled like the more modern version, so I couldn't twist the top off with my fingers.

This butter knife would have to do the trick.

I placed the edge of the knife between the top hinge and the tip of the pin, but I couldn't get the blade to slip through. I hissed, tired of everything working against me.

Removing my hand from the toilet paper on my head, I waited to see if it would fall. It stayed, as I'd been hoping from the few times I'd seen my stepdad treat a razor cut.

I hit the butt of the knife with my fist and wedged the blade between the hinge and pin, but not enough, and it hurt like the dickens. I couldn't hit it any harder. I needed something to use like a hammer...like the table legs.

Moving as quickly as possible, I snatched one wooden leg from where I'd tossed it on the bed and moved back to the hinge. This time, I held the butter knife at the base of the handle and smacked it repeatedly with the leg. The pin started to lift away from the hinge.

My stomach fluttered, and my senses sharpened. I

might make it out of here. I worked diligently while listening for the rumble of the engine, and soon, I was yanking the hinge out.

I got to work on the middle one.

The process felt as if it took forever, but when I finally got the bottom one loose, I could hardly believe it.

With all three pins removed, I stood back and examined the door. I had to separate the hinge so I could get through the opening. I placed my thumb on the top part of the hinge with my fingers underneath it, pulling it toward me. It wasn't easy, but I gritted my teeth and yanked harder, and finally, the hinge separated.

I followed the same process for the middle and bottom ones, and I had the door open enough to slide through. I glanced out the bedroom window to see it was pitch black outside. It'd taken longer than I'd realized, but our kidnapper wasn't back yet. I had time to try to get Saphira out.

Head pounding, I stepped into the hallway.

A faint rumbling hit my ears.

Our kidnapper had returned.

CHAPTER NINE

I FROZE. Everything inside me screamed to get Saphira out, but there was no time. It had taken me all evening to get myself out, and she was in a dragon-proof, metal-encased room.

The rumbling grew louder. It was definitely the truck from earlier and not someone driving by. Our kidnapper was almost back. I had to escape *now*, or all of this would have been for nothing. Once he saw how I'd broken out, I wouldn't have another opportunity.

Counting on Saphira's superb hearing, I said, "I'm sorry. He's almost back, and I've got to leave, but I *promise* I'll bring help."

A small bang on the door was the only response I could hear. The lack of frantic loudness led me to believe she was giving me permission.

With every passing second, he grew closer. The dragon was already so much stronger and faster than me. I needed a head start.

I ran to the end of the hallway. To my left was the

front door with a small rectangular window that revealed headlights flickering between tree branches. Adrenaline coursed harder through my blood, making the engine sound louder, as if I were in tune with my surroundings.

Pivoting right, I rushed into a den. The dark charcoal walls gave the place a more modern feel, and two black futons were the only furniture. This couldn't be where he lived.

My eyes found a white-painted back door with a window at the top revealing more of the looming forest.

There was my exit!

I held my breath as I turned the lock. *Please don't let this set off an alarm.* When it clicked, I exhaled and threw open the door. I stepped out onto a small cement porch, and my shoulders relaxed when no alarm blared to notify him of my escape. I forced myself to pause and shut the door, not wanting to alert him right away that I'd left. I needed as much time as possible before he began to hunt for me.

A shiver ran down my spine as the door shut. Then I was sprinting over the grass, the soggy earth underneath already clumping between my toes.

Gross. I hated being barefoot, but high heels would have impeded me more.

Rain still poured from the sky, and my shorts and shirt were drenched before I reached the tree line. Maybe this weather would help me. The rain should hide my noises and scent.

As I reached a Fraser fir, I pushed myself harder, racing into the woods. The engine was now loud. He'd be at the house momentarily and heading inside.

With every step, my feet sank into the ground, making

it hard to gain traction. This must be what quicksand felt like, but at least I could move forward.

My breathing was rapid, and I tried to get it under control. I didn't know which way was north, south, east, or west. I'd never gone camping and had always brushed off learning survival skills—and boy, did it show. I needed to find a road or someone's home.

Scurrying noises had my heart stopping. I'd been so focused on escaping that I'd forgotten about wildlife. I reminded myself what I'd learned during my time volunteering at a veterinary office: most animals took cover from the rain, just like humans, so this weather made the woods safer for me.

I paused to get my bearings. The heavy rain and darkness made it hard to see much farther than a few feet in front of me. I'd have to run until I found something to follow. Staying put wasn't an option.

Something charged at me, and I clamped my hands over my mouth to hold in a scream. *This is it. I'm going to die.*

A squirrel rushed by me to a tree for shelter.

I let out a maniacal laugh. I was letting my anxiety get the best of me. People went hiking all the time, and most of them made it out alive. I was being a drama queen.

A thick branch lay at the foot of a red spruce, and I snatched it up to carry as a weapon.

No more being scared of squirrels unless they shift into humans, I chastised myself. I was letting fear control me. I had to get away, send help for Saphira, and find my way back to Eva and Elliott. If I could convince them to leave with me, maybe the three of us could start fresh somewhere Drake could never find us. And if they refused to leave my stepdad, I guessed I'd deal with Peter as long as it kept us all safe.

That was worth risking everything. If I was going down, it would be swinging and not as some pathetic martyr.

From not too far away, I heard the door of the truck close. Shit, I hadn't made it very far, and he was already out of the vehicle.

I picked up my pace, trying my best to navigate the weeds and ground cover. Every few steps, a twig or rock stabbed me, but I gritted my teeth and refused to give up. I kept hoping my eyes would adjust to the darkness, but they hadn't. I began to move more quickly and focused on the ground right in front of me, dodging trees. I wanted to run, but I couldn't risk being careless.

"Everly!" a deep, sensuous voice called from behind me.

I startled and clamped my hands over my mouth to hold in my scream, forgetting I held that branch. It cut my lips, but I didn't feel the pain. *He* knew I was gone.

I had to go.

I pumped my arms and hurried, trying to prevent the branch from hitting me as I ran. I stumbled over a hidden root as the rain slanted, hammering my face. Lovely. Yet another hindrance that would make things more challenging. But that was the one thing that drove me—a challenge. And I'd be damned if I gave up now.

I got into a rhythm and only tripped over my feet every few steps. The rushing of a stream caught my attention, and I turned toward it. I'd read something about following a stream when you were lost in the woods. Water ran downhill, and I needed to remain at least a hundred feet away to reduce the chances of meeting wildlife, slipping, or running off a cliff.

As I made my way toward the water, an uncomfortably tight sensation shifted inside me. Something was definitely wrong, and I didn't need to be a genius to know what. I was being hunted.

The feeling of being prey once more twisted through my stomach. My hands shook, but I didn't slow. He would only catch me faster.

The sound of rocks jostling came from the direction of the water. With the loud noises, I imagined it was a large animal—like a bear.

I stayed on my path and didn't move any closer to the water. A stitch flared in my side, the pain worsening with every step. I was extremely out of shape, but I couldn't afford to stop and rest. Though he hadn't called out again, I could sense he was near.

I inhaled through my nose and breathed out of my mouth to see if that would calm my nerves and ease the discomfort. One time, a gym instructor had recommended that I hold my hands over my head to catch my breath faster, so that's exactly what I did. There was no point in worrying about looking stupid now.

Surprisingly, the tactic worked, and it also blocked a bit of the rain from hitting my face.

Despite my attempt to keep the same distance from the stream, I broke through the trees, and the bank came into view. It had cut to the right and intersected my path. That was what I got for having human ears in a torrential rainfall.

The stream was sizable, likely due to all the rain, and rocks led down to the water. Every ten to fifteen feet, the stream dropped down a short hill.

Under normal circumstances, I would have marveled at the sight. It was worthy of a painting. But now was *not* the time for inspiration.

I turned right to keep a hundred feet between me and the stream, but a tree branch just above my head shook. I screamed and dodged left, desperate to get away from whatever was about to attack me.

"Everly!" my kidnapper yelled. "I'm coming."

His words added to my fear, and tears ran down my face, mixing with the rain. An owl flew from the branch above me, not some evil raccoon desperate to eat me.

Now he had a better sense of where I was.

My foot hit smooth stone and slipped. I tumbled to the ground, and my knees hit rock, scraping off skin. I groaned as the sharp pain took hold, and I tried to get up but only slipped again.

This couldn't be happening. I had to get out of here. Gritting my teeth, I released the branch and forced myself to get slowly to my feet, ignoring the agony in my knees. I inched toward the muddy, twiggy ground and away from the slick, smooth rocks.

Once on solid footing, I hurried ahead, knees aching.

I touched the tree trunks to steady myself. I had to keep a level head, or I'd wind up hurt worse than I already was, no kidnapper needed.

The stream rushed beside me, and I made sure to keep it in view. After a few minutes, the sound of loud, crashing water made a lump form in my throat.

I knew that sound all too well. A waterfall.

As if confirming my thoughts, the trees broke away, revealing the drop-off. I couldn't see how far down it went. I'd have to find a way down from here.

Reaching the edge of the cliff, I clung to the trunk of a

fir and glanced over. Jagged boulders framed the waterfall. I'd have to go down using the trees. It would take a while, and the drop was steep, but it was nothing like the rocky waterfall on my left.

But as I moved deeper into the trees and away from the water, the earth under my feet crumbled away. I tried to jump back onto solid ground, and I gripped a tree trunk, the wood rough beneath my fingers. As my hands slipped, splinters cut into my palms. I wasn't strong enough to hold on, and I couldn't get any purchase with my feet. I yelled, "Help!" At least, if the kidnapper found me, I wouldn't fall. All my life, I'd tried to do things the smart way, and here I was, about to die in a mudslide.

"I'm almost there!" he exclaimed, sounding concerned.

Or maybe I was delusional.

"I can't hold on!" I exclaimed as my grip slipped.

Sky blue eyes appeared through the darkness just as my fingers slid from the trunk.

"Everly!" he yelled as I fell.

I tumbled backward down the incline. Rocks dug into my skin, and dirt crumbled around me. I threw my body out of its backward roll, but I lurched sideways and kept sliding, hitting what felt like every rock and branch in my path.

My body slammed into something, and the back of my head took the brunt of the impact. Bright sparks and then black spots flashed across my vision.

Through my blurry gaze, I saw the shape of my kidnapper running down the incline. Where I'd slipped and fallen, he expertly navigated the terrain. He hunkered down next to me, and my vision narrowed to a pinpoint.

His gorgeous blue eyes were the last image I'd ever see.

He brushed my hair away from my face and whispered, "I've got you, Everly. I'll save you."

For some reason, I believed he would.

CHAPTER TEN

DARKNESS SURROUNDED ME. I was dying. I kept waiting for the blinding light that people saw during near-death experiences, but it never came. I'd thought running through the dark, rainy woods had been the bleakest moment of my life, but that was nothing compared to being submerged in unending darkness.

I couldn't see my hands or body, and it felt like there was nothing around me.

Maybe I wasn't in a physical form.

Something brushed against my face, but as I reached up to touch the sensation, all I felt was air.

I tried to move my legs, but nothing happened. Fear settled heavily inside me.

A tickle started somewhere within. The sensation spread throughout my...existence? Because I no longer had a body.

No matter what I did, I couldn't get away, and the tickle strengthened into a tingling sensation. The odd sensation was hot, uncomfortably so, but maybe that was from my body temperature dropping after getting soaked by the rain in the dark.

I had to be dying, and my subconscious was the only thing processing the stimuli. What should have been my chest tightened at the realization, and I'd have done anything to caress the bracelet my mom had given me.

Scorching heat swirled through me. I wondered if the kidnapper had changed into his dragon form and was breathing fire on me. That would be one hell of a convenient way for him to hide dead bodies.

Flames licked through me, racing toward something deep inside.

My heart.

Maybe this was what being burned alive felt like when you were unconscious. No one could endure something like this and live to tell the story. I'd never believed in a higher power, but with the agony searing through me, I was ready to plead and beg someone, *anyone*, to take this misery away.

Then something *snapped* inside me, and my consciousness slipped away.

A BANGING REPEATED in sync with the throbbing in my head. Something else pressed into my back, and I fidgeted, too tired to even attempt to open my eyes.

Faint footsteps sounded, and a deep, sexy voice said, "Cut it out. She's *fine* but needs rest."

"What did you do to her?" a strong female voice replied, sounding very similar to Saphira. "If you put so much as a *bruise* on her, I'll kill you when I get out of this prison cell."

The past several days replayed in my mind, and any hope of getting more rest vanished. The memory of tumbling down the steep incline and banging my head had my eyes popping open.

I shouldn't be alive.

The world swirled in front of me, and I sat up so quickly that I nearly tumbled to the floor. My clothes clung to me, still drenched from the rain, and the scent of copper almost had me dry-heaving. I scanned the room I'd escaped not long ago, searching for the horrible smell, but nothing stood out. The room looked the same but also different.

Shaking my head, I closed my eyes and opened them again, but the view didn't change. The room was more detailed with elements I hadn't noticed before. The dark charcoal walls were actually several individual colors swirled together—black and white with faint touches of orange and yellow to provide warmth. Everything that a true painter knows, but never had I seen colors quite like this.

There was only one explanation—a brain injury. I needed to get to a hospital quickly. I wasn't sure how I'd survived this long.

When I touched the back of my head where it had hit the trunk, there was only mild discomfort.

"I didn't hurt her, for gods' sake," our kidnapper replied. His voice was sexier than I remembered, the sound alone calling to something deep inside me.

Something brushed against my mind, and I jumped to my feet and turned around, searching for the danger, but nothing was there. The room spun faster than it should have, and I noticed a tiny spider hiding in the far corner twenty feet away. It wasn't much larger than a pen tip, but I could make out all eight legs.

A strangled groan left me as my heart pounded.

Footsteps hurried toward me, and my attention swung to the doorway. My kidnapper stepped in...and my heart stopped as the world tilted on its axis.

There was a hint of a scar on his chin, something I hadn't noticed before, and it added to his rugged good looks. His sky blue eyes were even more breathtaking with the white and blue shades so beautiful. I could stare into his eyes for the rest of my life and never grow tired of them.

He lifted his hands as if he were approaching a rabid animal. "Everly, you're safe."

I laughed, not sure why. The sound wasn't normal, and it echoed as if I were in *someone else's* body. Something was very wrong.

I took several steps back until I hit the wall behind me. "I need a hospital." The person who'd spoken sounded elegant and scared. The scared part fit me perfectly, but not the elegant part.

"No, you don't." He shook his head and took one step closer. "That's the last thing you want. Trust me."

Rage blazed through my blood as I clenched my jaw. "*I* just finished a premed degree. Did you?"

He opened his mouth to respond, but I wasn't done.

"I *know* I shouldn't be standing right now, but I am. I'm seeing colors I never knew existed, and I can see a fucking millimeter-big spider in great detail across the room! So please forgive me if I don't *trust you*. I'm *here* because of you."

Hanging his head, he kept his attention locked on me. "That's fair. You're right."

Something inside tugged at me to close the distance between us and tell him it was okay, almost like I had a split personality. I reached for my bracelet, but all I felt was my skin. The bracelet was gone. A sob built in my chest.

"Hey. Wait." He reached into his jeans pocket and pulled out the bracelet. "It's right here."

The asshole had taken it from me again. Even though I was angry at him, I also wanted to kiss him. Something was truly off with me. "Give it back," I demanded, sounding like a petulant child.

"I will, but don't put it on." He tossed the bracelet to me.

It came at me in slower motion than normal, and I easily caught it as something brushed against my mind again.

Clasping my fingers around the bracelet, I breathed rapidly, not even upset that he'd told me not to wear it. "Something is seriously wrong with me. Things are moving slower, and I can feel something weird inside. I've injured my brain and need medical help."

He pinched the bridge of his nose, and his brows furrowed.

The overwhelming urge to rub my fingers over the indentation and smooth out his worry had me taking an involuntary step forward. Oh, *hell*, no. I had to get my act together.

"Everly," he breathed. The sound was like a paint-brush running over a blank canvas—magical and full of promise.

My body warmed in a way that was inappropriate and foreign to me. Ever since Mom's death, I'd vowed to stay away from men and focus on my studies. And though my captor was delectable, he would *not* tempt me. I clenched my free hand and chanted internally, *Go away, Stockholm syndrome.*

"You fell and got hurt," he said, moving another foot closer to me.

Some of the warmth froze, and I sneered. "Yeah, I was there and *experienced* it. The tree won, which is why—"

"I *couldn't* take you to a hospital." His irises darkened, and he rasped, "You wouldn't have made it. Your skull was cracked. When I examined it to see how bad it was, I changed you."

My heart pounded like the drums of war. I had no idea what he meant, and I didn't want to. Whatever he'd done was why I was feeling so strange. However, I refused to ignore my problems. Denial often made a situation unsalvageable. "What does that mean?"

Licking his lips, he lifted his chin as if he was ready to face me head-on. Sweat pooled under my arms.

"I..." He blinked for a long moment.

If he didn't spit it out, I'd be forced to rush over there and rip his clothes off to show him who was boss. I froze, my sexually infused trigger startling some sanity back into me so I didn't follow through on that threat. I'd been attracted to men before, and I'd never had trouble keeping my mind focused. Why was I struggling with *him*? Maybe it was the near-death experience.

He cleared his throat. "I turned you into a dragon shifter."

I stood there, dumbfounded. Pressure built inside until I might explode. I examined my exposed skin for a bite. All I could see were cuts and bruises where twigs and rocks had hit me, but nothing that looked like teeth marks. I ran my fingers along my neck, searching for puncture wounds, but all I felt was smooth skin.

He inched closer to me. "What are you doing?"

"Stay back." I threw my hands forward, making sure the one still held the bracelet. That was when I noticed blood on my hands from where I'd touched the base of my neck. They shook as I turned my palms toward me. Blood stained them, too. "Did you bite me on my scalp?"

"What?" he asked loudly.

I jumped back, hitting my head on the wall supporting me. A twinge of discomfort wafted through me but disappeared.

That wasn't possible...for a human. But I wasn't human anymore.

"Shit. Sorry." He groaned. "I'm not trying to upset you, but you caught me off guard. You can't change someone by biting them. The blood is from your head injury."

The last part was the only thing that made actual sense. Though learning he hadn't bitten me eased some of my tension, lightheadedness swept in. "Then *how* am I a *dragon*?" The last word came out in a squeak.

"It's a special ability I have. I couldn't let you die." He blew out a breath. "So I changed you."

"You didn't ask for my permission!" I wiped the blood on my shorts and clutched my bracelet tightly, needing something to ground me. Mom always did that, and I needed any part of her I could find at that moment.

My captor flinched. "True, but I couldn't. You were unconscious and dying."

"That doesn't make this *okay*." All my life, the only thing I'd had of my own were my choices: what degree I wanted, where to go to school, and whether to keep in touch with my brother and sister. I didn't have close friends, a loving family, or someone to confide in. And the one thing I could count on—making decisions for myself—had been stripped away by someone who'd made the largest decision possible for me.

He laughed, and the cruelness on his face yanked at something deep inside. I'd hurt him, and I wanted to ease his pain, which wasn't rational. I dug my feet into the hardwood, refusing to budge from my spot.

"You want to be a doctor." He waved a hand toward me and stalked forward, a dangerous edge to his glare. "You're telling me that if a patient was dying, and you could save them, you *wouldn't* unless they gave you permission?"

I straightened my back. "They'd be in a hospital, so that would be my permission."

"Not if they were in a wreck and were found unconscious. Or what if you stumbled upon someone struggling in a park?" His jaw twitched as his pupils slitted.

He said something else, but I couldn't hear it. All I could do was stare at his dragon peeping through. When his pupils had slitted before, it had terrified me, but now I was intrigued...uncomfortably so.

He growled, "Would you? Answer me."

I shook my head, trying to focus on the conversation and not him. He was so close I could feel the warmth wafting from his body and breathe in his delicious minty-amber scent. "Yes, I would, but I wouldn't be changing them fundamentally."

"I'd rather you *hate* me than be *dead*," he said with conviction.

"Oh, don't worry. I've hated you since you attacked our car." I was done letting him bully me. "You're going to kill us, anyway. Don't pretend. We've seen your face. You can't let us go. You might as well tell me your name. There's no reason to hold back now."

"Thorn," he murmured. "My name is Thorn, and I won't kill you. Either of you. Why would you think that?"

"Don't you dare play the good-guy angle again." I stuck my finger in his chest, and something *zapped* between us.

He gasped, feeling the sensation, too, but I schooled my features into a mask of indifference. My expression was one thing I was good at controlling. I'd learned to do it after losing Mom so I wouldn't anger my stepdad with looks of hurt or disgust.

"You, *Thorn*, kidnapped Saphira and me, locked us up, chased after me when I tried to escape, then changed me into a *dragon*." I let my anger flow through every word, wanting him to feel how much I despised what he'd done. "You are *not* a nice guy. You're a *monster*."

His lip curled, and pain flashed across his face. His eyes turned cold. "Let me show you a monster." He yanked my arm, dragging me into the hallway.

I planted my feet on the hardwood, trying to fight his hold, but he was too strong.

Terrified, I wondered what I'd unleashed.

CHAPTER ELEVEN

NO MATTER WHAT I DID, Thorn was too strong to stop. I could have still been human with how easily he was dragging me through the living room and back down the hall. His fingers dug into my skin, adding more discomfort to the electricity sizzling between us. The pain was as agonizing as it was pleasurable.

"What are you doing?" I rasped, trying to yank out of his hold.

I might as well have been a baby doll because he didn't even miss a step and continued moving at the same quick stride.

"If you want to be a prisoner, you'll be one," he growled.

My throat hurt as my legs gave out. I fell to my knees, and with one swoop, he picked me up and carried me around the turn in the hall.

The door to the room I'd been staying in was exactly how I'd left it. It hung crookedly in the doorway, each hinge still undone. I wasn't sure what he thought putting me back in there would accomplish, but then he walked past it to the last door in the hall.

Saphira.

"What are you doing to her?" Saphira shouted and banged on the wall.

Instead of responding, he dropped me and pulled out the key to unlock her door.

This was my last chance to get out of here, and I had to try.

I leaped away just as his hand grabbed for me and caught my hair. The door clicked open, and he yanked on me, setting my scalp on fire.

"Shit!" he hissed, and let go, then promptly caressed the base of my skull where it had hit the tree trunk.

My eyes burned with tears. As the door opened, he wrapped his free hand around my waist and threw me inside. Saphira yelped and jumped away, and I sailed onto her mattress.

Before I could even glower at him, the door had slammed shut, the sound echoing over the metal. I yelled, "Asshole!" feeling a lot braver with him on the other side of the door.

"Everly!" Saphira hurried to me. "You're hurt!" She reached out to inspect my skull, her eyes wide with concern.

Her worry caused my tears to break free and stream down my face. No one had even pretended to care about me in so long that even though she'd been willingly taking me to Drake to become his breeder, I couldn't stay mad at her.

That was how pathetic I'd become.

I caught her hand and shook my head. "I'm fine. Thorn saved me."

Her eyes bulged, and she stumbled away from me and into the wall next to the door.

With everything Thorn had done, including tossing me in here so cruelly, I couldn't blame her disbelief. "I know. I was surprised that he saved me, too, but he needs me for *something*."

Her smooth, dark skin blanched, and she lifted a shaky finger. "Who the *hell* are you?"

I stood, not wanting my clothes to soak the sheets and because her reaction had unsettled me. "What do you mean, who am I? You picked me up from my stepdad's house yesterday."

"No." Saphira jerked her head from side to side. "You look and sound just like Everly, but you aren't human."

Was that what was tripping her up? I rubbed my hands together, needing to expel my nervous energy. "I *know*," I croaked. "I escaped from the room and ran into the woods. I tried to get away, but I slid down a huge incline and cracked my skull. I should be dead, but Thorn found me, and I woke up like *this*." I waved a hand in front of my body. "My vision is funny, I'm hearing things, and there's something messing with my mind. He said he had to change me to save me." Maybe I was supposed to die, and this was me cheating death.

"That's *insane*." Saphira raised a hand and held it in front of her. "We're born as dragon shifters, not *turned*. Stop with whatever *game* this is, and tell me how you were able to hide your dragon before!"

None of this made sense. Thorn had told me he'd changed me, and now she was saying that wasn't possible. I wasn't sure who to believe. Each of them had a reason to lie to me.

Just when I thought someone cared about me, I was

proven wrong. If that wasn't proof that I was destined to be alone, I wasn't sure what was. "I wasn't hiding anything." I was so tired of trying to be enough for everyone. Maybe that was the point—I needed to be content with myself from here on out. "But believe what you want. I don't care."

I glanced down at my soaked shirt and shorts. Blood stained the shoulders of my white lace top, and the bottom half was covered in mud. My black shorts had mud caked on them as well, and I looked like a drowned rat.

The panel in the door opened, and clothes were dropped onto the floor, followed by two towels.

Thorn cleared his throat. "I know I said I'd be a monster, but Everly needs to take a shower after her *outing*, and there's extra there for Saphira. The clothes will be too large for Everly since she's short, but she can roll them up to an acceptable length."

I wanted to wave my middle finger high in the hopes he'd see it, but getting out of these soaked, muddy clothes sounded too good to pass up.

I approached the clothes as if they were a weapon, making sure there weren't any surprises. All I found were two thin, white cotton towels, two pairs of women's sweatpants—one gray and one black—and two medium black cotton shirts.

Something twisted hard in my stomach. Where the hell had he gotten these women's clothes? Worse, why did it bother me that he might have a girlfriend or a *wife*? My breathing quickened as anger slammed through me, and something sulfuric lodged in my throat.

"Whoa!" Saphira exclaimed and lifted her hands. "You need to calm down."

Oh? *Now*, when I was barely hanging on to my sanity, she decided to talk to me. That same odd feeling brushed against my mind and roared.

Something growled nearby, and I staggered back a few steps, trying to locate the threat and get away. I couldn't find it, despite the growling growing louder.

"Holy gods. You weren't lying." Saphira gasped and hunkered down. "Everly, you need to calm down, or you will attempt to shift, which is impossible in this room and will only drive your new dragon crazy."

Shift.

The new, foreign part of me—the part that roared —*really* enjoyed the sound of it.

"You're angry, hurt, or scared. Hell, from what you told me, you're most likely all three, and it's causing your dragon to want to take control." She spoke slowly and calmly, reminding me of when Mom would sing the twins a lullaby to calm them and get them to sleep. "I need you to breathe slowly and deeply. Clear your mind, and take yourself to a happy place."

For a second, I felt like I was listening to a clip from *Peter Pan*. But instead of flying, I was trying to stay...human.

I kind of wished it were the pixie dust issue instead.

The heat in my throat strengthened, and I opened my mouth, only for smoke to trickle out. *I'm breathing out black smoke*. She hadn't been exaggerating. I would shift if I didn't get it together.

The panel opened again, and those breathtaking eyes locked on me through the hole. "Everly!" His voice was filled with fear.

"Don't come in here," Saphira said. "You'll make it worse. I need her to focus on something *happy*, *not* our *kidnapper* who got us into this mess. If she attempts to shift in here, it's going to be very problematic."

His eyes had a calming effect on me. I stared into them and focused on how it had felt to paint during the past several days. Though I'd been under pressure to make money, there'd been something freeing about it. To see something blank come to life with whatever image I envisioned had brought *me* to life for that short time.

The dark purples I loved to use for the sky flitted through my mind, reminding me of Thorn's scales. The various blues and whites I'd used to capture the essence of the city skyline were similar to my kidnapper's eyes.

"You're doing it," Saphira encouraged. "Keep it up."

Her voice brought me back to the present. The roaring wasn't in my head anymore, and the smoke had gone. Instead of anger, I felt exhausted. "Thank you."

"You're welcome." Saphira forced a smile, though it didn't reach her eyes. "Why don't you take a shower and clean up? It might make you feel..." She trailed off, searching for the right word, then settled on, "Better."

I wondered what word she'd been about to use, but it didn't matter. A shower would give me some alone time to begin to deal with my new fate.

I bent down and snatched a towel, the black sweatpants, and a shirt. The idea of blending into the darkness was alluring.

Although...now that I had dragon vision, that would be impossible, much to my chagrin.

I headed to the tiny bathroom, seeking isolation. As I turned to shut the door, my traitorous gaze landed on him.

He was still watching me.

Something inside me vibrated like a cat purring, and a

lightness filled my chest. Two very strong reactions that *he* shouldn't inspire.

Once I shut the door, I leaned my head against the wood and breathed. I put the bracelet on my wrist, not wanting to lose it again.

There was movement in the outer room, followed by Saphira murmuring, "How did you make her a dragon?"

That was an answer I would also like to know, and I held my breath.

Instead of words, I heard the door panel slide shut. That was answer enough—he wasn't going to tell her.

I slumped and forced myself to turn on the plastic-walled shower. As soon as I could, I stepped into the hot water and washed my concerns and fear away.

I WASN'T sure how long I remained in the shower. The water never rose to a warmth I enjoyed, and even though I tried like hell to focus on getting clean, I couldn't get the demons that plagued me out of my mind.

My only reprieve was the long stretch of solitude.

I towel-dried my hair, the back of my skull still tender. I couldn't fathom how I'd survived. The injury I'd sustained should've left me incoherent for days. But here I stood, brushing my wet hair with my fingers, unsure how I looked because there was no mirror.

I quickly pulled on the clothes Thorn had set out for me. Disgust with myself settled hard in my stomach as I pathetically smelled them, wondering if I could pick up the scent of the person they belonged to.

They didn't smell like anything except Thorn, from when he had handled them.

The clothing was a size too large for me and definitely too long, as he'd suspected. My heart fluttered at the fact that he'd paid enough attention to me to notice, forcing me to get angry at myself. I would *not* allow myself to feel soft, warm feelings toward a man who'd done nothing but hurt me.

Footsteps padded to the bathroom door, and I opened it before Saphira could knock. I didn't want her accusing me of anything else or asking more questions I couldn't answer. It would only frustrate the both of us.

I forced a smile, but when she flinched, I figured it hadn't hit the mark. Mom had told me to fake it until I made it, and I'd been taking that piece of advice ever since I'd left her grave.

"Your turn," I said, trying to sound happy.

She narrowed her eyes and brushed past me. She glanced around the bathroom, and I followed her gaze.

Steam rolled out of the tiny room, and the lights were off. I realized I'd showered in the dark. The steam wasn't an anomaly, except the shower had felt cool the entire time, so that much steam seemed weird. The darkness was most definitely not normal...not for me.

"I'm assuming you're okay with sharing the bed again?" She arched her brow. "Otherwise, one of us is sleeping on the floor."

I shrugged. "We might as well get comfortable with each other. We might be here for a while." He couldn't put me back in the other room because I was a dragon shifter now. I was stuck in this aluminum can with her.

"That's what I was thinking," she agreed before shutting the door.

I went to the bed and stared at the mud-stained sheet. At least it was the sheet and not the mattress cover. I removed it from the bed just as the lock on the bedroom door clicked.

Thorn was back. The door swung open, revealing him with a new blue sheet, pillow, and a lavender blanket. My throat tightened.

He had changed into gray sweatpants that left very little to the imagination, and his white cotton shirt hugged his body, each curve of muscle on full display. If I wasn't careful, drool might run from the corner of my mouth.

He stayed in the doorway and held out the items. "Here, I thought you might want some clean stuff since I kinda threw you on the bed." Regret lined his face.

"That isn't very monstrous of you," I said as I took the items from him. "Or are they lined with itching powder or something to hurt us?"

"I am *not* going to hurt you." He placed a hand on his chest and stepped closer to me.

Electricity surged between us, leaving me breathless.

"I promise." His eyes locked on my lips. "That was never my intention, especially not now."

The last three words replayed in my head, but my mind couldn't focus. I edged toward him, each of us drawn to the other like magnets.

"Why did you take me?" Something inside me was desperate for him, but I couldn't want someone who could be so careless.

"Because—" he started, but the bathroom door opened.

CHAPTER TWELVE

THE ROAR RANG in my head again as both parts of me were angry over the interruption. I was desperate to know *why* Thorn had taken me, and I was damn close to getting the answer.

Thorn took a hurried step away as if we hadn't shared some sort of inappropriate moment.

"Did I interrupt something?" Saphira asked, and I looked at her to find her gorgeous skin back to its normal brown color and her face scrunched in puzzlement.

The clothes hugged her body. One size too small, they fit her like a glove, as if she purposely wanted to show off her figure. I wanted to shove her back into the bathroom and slam the door. She was captivating—worthy of painting. I didn't doubt where Thorn's attention would be now. I couldn't compete with her.

Not that I was *trying* to compete. I had to get my head on straight.

"I was just dropping off clean sheets," Thorn rasped.

Oh, I bet I knew why his voice was gravelly. My jaw

ached from clenching my teeth. My stomach burned, and my attention darted to Thorn.

The burning was extinguished as quickly as it had come.

His eyes were locked on me, his pupils slitted, and my heart jump-started, calming the crazy whirlwind of emotions.

"And you were about to tell me why you kidnapped me." I wouldn't let him off the hook. If I didn't push, I would never gain clarity. I moved so I could shift my attention between him and Saphira. The last thing I needed was for them to realize I was attracted to *him*. One, he could use that to his advantage if he wasn't already, and two, I didn't want Saphira to judge me more than she already had.

Saphira crossed her arms, enhancing her chest, and a snarl rang inside my head. She shook her head. "There's a far more pressing question. How the *hell* did you turn her into a dragon shifter? Do you realize what you've done?"

Thorn's gaze ripped from me to her. Instead of desire, though, his face turned pink, and his nostrils flared. "Yes, I do. I *saved* her. Would you rather I had let her die?"

I swallowed. He had saved me, but I didn't need to believe he was a hero. If he hadn't kidnapped us, I wouldn't have almost died.

My heart dropped at the thought of him not taking us. What the *hell* was *wrong* with me?

"I'm not buying it." She lifted her chin and sneered. "You took us against our will. I don't believe you give a shit what happens to us. You need to keep her alive for whatever your plan is."

"Says the woman who was willing to take Everly to a dragon shifter so she could be his human breeder." Thorn wrinkled his nose as he spat, "At least I've put off that horrible future."

Put off. Not *ended.* The wording was particular.

My insides ached at the thought of him leaving me.

No, it had to be heartburn. I *didn't* like this sexy man —er—man. *Just man.* Not sexy. *Ugh, Everly, keep your head on straight. Don't let your hormones get the best of you.* I'd never had this problem before, and of all the times and places, I'd rather it not be *here* with *him.*

Needing to prove to myself I hadn't completely lost it, I straightened my shoulders. "You're deflecting instead of answering her question. How did you change me? You said it wasn't a bite. Was it a scratch?" It had to involve the mixing of bodily fluids or a virus or whatever it was that made someone a dragon shifter.

The corners of his mouth tipped upward as his attention settled back on me. His face softened as he said, "No, it wasn't a scratch, either. DNA doesn't make up a dragon shifter."

"Exactly!" Saphira exclaimed as she pointed a finger and marched to the bed. "That's why *this* shouldn't be possible. If I hadn't seen her nearly shift, I wouldn't have believed it. I would think you and she were in cahoots and had a witch involved, but she was terrified. That's something you can't fake. Drake and King Arman will be very intrigued when they learn what you did."

Thorn's face hardened, and an alarming glint appeared in his eye.

My body warmed from the danger he emanated.

"King *Arman* will know *exactly* what it means." His voice was deep and low, reminding me of the various red and orange shades I used in a painting to convey that type of emotion.

His hurt and anger called to something inside me. I hadn't noticed that I'd moved toward him until my hand touched his arm.

The electricity between us sprang to life, and I gasped at the pure intensity, as if his emotions had amplified our connection.

His irises glowed faintly, reminiscent of light breaking through the clouds on an overcast morning, as if my touch had given him peace or hope.

Then he flinched and jerked his arm away from me. His usual indifferent façade slipped back in place.

The rejection stung, and I dropped my hand as my face burned. I couldn't believe I'd tried to be there for him after everything he'd done, and worse, that he'd disregarded me.

Saphira's brows furrowed as she glanced between us, but before she could say something, he stepped toward the door.

"That's the beauty about this situation." He yanked open the door. "I don't have to give you anything. You eat when I allow it. You shower when I decide you can. Anything you want or desire has to come from me, and tonight, my generosity has ended." He stepped outside and shut the door, the sound echoing against the metal in the walls.

His absence caused my head to swim, as if he were the oxygen I needed. Unshed tears burned my eyes. He shouldn't have this effect on me.

"Asswipe," Saphira growled and banged a fist against the wall.

I could hear his footsteps in the hallway, but then he was gone. All I could do was stand there and breathe in the last of his scent before it vanished. Needing comfort, I wrapped my arms around myself.

"Help me make noise so we..." Saphira trailed off and looked at me. Her hand went still and dropped to her side.

Great. She must have realized that something even weirder was going on with me. I didn't have the energy to answer questions about why I found Thorn attractive, especially since I didn't understand it myself.

"Gods." She sighed and dropped her head. "You're a huge mess."

At her assessment, a tear streamed down my face. The truth hurt.

"I'm sorry," I whispered. I tried not to show emotion around others, but I couldn't get myself together. "I—"

"You do *not* need to apologize." Saphira smiled sadly as she removed the dirty sheet from the bed and unfolded the new one. "You haven't connected with your dragon, which is difficult to do at ten, let alone your age. You'll feel all sorts of crazy until we can get you outside so you can shift."

The hold on my heart loosened, and I wiped away the tear. "Wait. This is normal? I feel like I'm losing my mind."

Saphira plopped onto the side of the bed closest to the bathroom, grabbed the extra pillow, and placed it on my side. She patted the spot next to her. "It is normal. When you shift, you get to know your dragon. Right now, it's like there's this foreign entity in your body with its own emotions and thoughts because you haven't truly merged."

Thank goodness. I must have confused that struggle with my attraction to Thorn. I had a valid reason: I was misunderstanding my dragon. "Ugh. I don't know if I can go on like this much longer." I plopped onto the bed, reminding myself not to get too comfortable with Saphira even if I needed a friend. She had Drake's interests at heart, not mine. But she could provide me with insight to help me get a handle on my new dragon.

"It will be hard, but you'll manage." She pulled her hair to the side and lay back on her pillow. "I could tell you were strong the moment I met you and saw how your stepdad treated you."

Now that I knew how good her hearing was, I'd bet she'd heard Peter's words: *It's about time she was useful.* He'd never hidden that he didn't like my presence. "I wouldn't call it strong. I would call it learning to survive."

"They're one and the same to me." She shrugged as her wet hair turned the light blue pillowcase a shade darker.

"That's why you didn't have a problem handing me off to Drake?" The words were out before I could think them through. I usually didn't hold people accountable for their actions. It didn't actually change anything, besides making everyone uncomfortable. I liked standing out academically, not through confrontation.

She pursed her lips. "I honestly thought you knew what you were signing up for. I didn't realize he'd let you believe you were agreeing to marry him—a *human* him."

Now that I reflected on our past conversation, he hadn't. "He used words like *mine, belong,* and *heirs*. I just assumed that was what he meant."

"Please. If he left out the words *dragon shifter, breeder,* and *mistress,* knowing you were human and unaware of our world, then what else could you have thought?" Saphira rubbed her temples. "That's not okay.

In our world, agreements are binding, but he can't hold you to the agreement because he didn't disclose everything."

"It wasn't in writing." I shrugged. "So I'm not hopeful on getting out of it." That would've been smart of me to demand, but I wasn't one to confront people and protect myself when it came to my siblings—hence why I'd been taken advantage of by my stepdad and Drake.

Saphira cringed. "It doesn't matter if it's not in writing. An agreement can't be misleading, and *this* was. If we get out of here, I'll take you home."

My breath caught, and I tipped my head toward her. "Are you serious?" I hadn't expected her to go against Drake's wishes. He was also her prince.

"Of course." Saphira touched her chest. "He may be my future king, but that doesn't mean I have to go along with him when he's wrong. I thought he was doing questionable things before, but *this* confirms it, and he's gone too far. I'll get my dad to talk to King Arman and inform him of what Drake was trying to pull."

I didn't want to cause Saphira problems, but I didn't have a choice. "I appreciate what you're doing, but I can't go back. *If* we get out of here, I'll follow through on my promise, especially if an agreement is binding in your world."

"I told you we have a case for why it can't be upheld." Saphira rolled onto her side toward me and propped her head on her hand. "It'll be fine. We'll make sure to get the king involved."

"No, *you* don't understand." There was no doubt in my mind about what would happen if I didn't show up to take the role. "If I don't go, he'll take my sister instead."

"Why would you say that?" She shook her head. "I'm telling you—"

I already knew she was going to regurgitate that I'd be allowed out of the agreement. "Because my stepdad stole money from them. I heard the entire conversation Drake had with Peter. If my stepdad couldn't repay the money, Drake said he'd take my sister as payment."

Saphira's jaw dropped. "What? That's crazy. He was blackmailing a *human* for his daughter?"

"Yes, he was. When Drake left, I tried to talk to Peter. He wouldn't tell me anything, but the more I thought about Eva being forced into a loveless relationship…" I trailed off, the emotions clogging my throat. I jumped to my feet and paced in front of the door. "I couldn't allow that to happen."

I paused, chest heaving, trying not to melt down more than I already had.

Something pulsed through my veins like a jolt, and I had no doubt it was my dragon.

"Wait. If he wanted your sister, how did you get involved?" Saphira bit her bottom lip, looking like she was trying to solve a complicated math problem.

That part should've been obvious. "I remembered Peter talking about a bar that Drake owns downtown, so I went straight there and found Drake. I demanded he take me instead of Eva if we couldn't come up with the money. I thought I'd figure a way out of it. I even took paintings to my local art gallery, but not one of them sold. Then my time was up, and you showed up to take me to him."

"I asked him why a human would agree to his terms, and he just smiled, saying it was part of his charm." She closed her eyes. "I figured he'd promised you nice things in return. I had no clue he'd gotten *that* bad."

Footsteps pounded down the hallway toward us, but I couldn't seem to care. I was too focused on needing to convince her that none of that mattered. "Either way, I have to go to Drake. Otherwise, he'll take my sister." Then *all* of this would've been for nothing.

A loud growl came from behind the door, followed by a click. Thorn stepped inside, smoke trickling from his nose and his hands fisted at his sides.

My dragon roared in approval while I froze in terror.

CHAPTER THIRTEEN

EVEN THE PART of me that was terrified didn't want to tear my eyes away from Thorn. The image of him before me needed to be immortalized, and I tried desperately to capture the memory in detail so I could recall it later and do it justice.

"He *forced* you to be his?" he rasped, each word followed by a trickle of smoke from his mouth. "You weren't willing on your own?"

Saphira scoffed and sat upright, placing her body slightly in front of me on the bed. "Why does that matter to you?"

That was a valid question, but that foreign entity within me brushed against my mind, and the urge to grab a fistful of her hair and yank her out of my way surged through me.

Great, he'd blessed me with a violent dragon. What else could go wrong? I winced. Though I didn't believe in fate or anything else, for that matter, especially since there was no proof it existed in medicine or science, I didn't want to jinx myself. *I take it back*, I thought, sending that out to the universe just in case.

"That's none of *your* concern," he growled, and marched to my side of the bed. He hovered over me. "You were *forced* into this?" He searched my face for answers.

The heat from his body rolled over me, despite several feet separating us. My dragon calmed at his nearness and the fact that we had his attention.

His body quivered as his face twisted in a combination of anger and agony.

"Shit!" Saphira hissed and jumped to her feet. "Get yourself under control. You can't shift in here, and you'll wind up hurting us if your dragon goes crazy."

Somehow, I knew I was the reason he was out of control. "Yes and no. Technically, it was my sister, but she just turned eighteen, and I promised my mom on her deathbed that I would protect her and my brother. I had to take her place."

His breathing slowed, and his face smoothed. I sort of wished he could shift in here. I wanted to witness him shifting into his dragon form because it would be mind-blowing.

"So...you don't have feelings for him?" he murmured.

If I'd been just human, I wouldn't have heard the question. Even now, his words sounded like a rush of wind. "No," I answered loudly and scrunched my nose. "His personality ruins everything about him."

"Why is that relevant?" Saphira placed her hands on her hips. "It doesn't matter if she finds him attractive. She agreed to take her sister's place."

A snarl vibrated deep in his chest as he glared at her. His jaw twitched as he spoke through gritted teeth, "It matters because he's forced a *human* into our world against her will. I see that his ethics don't fall far from the *king's*." He said the last word as if it were vile.

"Well, it's not a problem anymore." Saphira gestured to me. "Because she's not human. And the king is *nothing* like his son."

Thorn laughed bitterly. "That's what he wants you to believe."

Despite the anger and malice lacing his words, there was a hint of heartbreak, too. If I hadn't heard that tone enough in my own voice over the years, I wouldn't have picked up on it, but the sound tugged at something deep inside me. I threw my legs over the bed and leaned toward him, catching myself before I reached for him.

My reaction to him perplexed me. When I met him, I'd found him handsome, and he had intrigued me, but ever since I'd changed, it was like I *needed* him. It had to be a type of sire bond. All the vampire and a few werewolf shows and books talked about that, so it made sense that it would happen with dragons.

"I *know* the royal family." Saphira lifted her chin, staring down her nose at Thorn. "I grew up around them. My father is the king's trusted advisor, so don't act like I'm misinformed. Your opinion of them stems from your own ill-perceived views."

"Ill-perceived?" Thorn grimaced. Anger and hurt were etched into his face. "I can promise you that is *not* the case."

Whatever had happened to him was personal. I wasn't sure how I knew that, but something inside me screamed it was true.

Saphira fisted her hands. "I don't have anything to prove to you. Obviously, you aren't willing to see reason." She raced toward the unlocked door, trying to escape.

I'd been expecting it to happen. If she got out of here, she could lock Thorn and me in the room while she went to get Drake.

I should have joined her, but I didn't budge. It was as if my survival skills had vanished into thin air.

Thorn didn't waste a second. He rushed after her.

As Saphira reached for the doorknob, Thorn slammed into her side, knocking her into the wall.

He planted himself in front of the door, blocking her escape. His pupils slitted as he shook his head, frowning. "And here I was, hoping you actually *wanted* to listen to my story to see if there was any truth to it."

She groaned and rubbed the right side of her arm. Wet hair stuck to her face, making her seem less elegant than usual.

"Yeah, I'm the misguided one." He snorted and tromped to the door. "I'm done talking." As he opened the door, his gaze settled on me, and he said gently, "Get some rest. The tenderness in your head should be gone by morning if you get a solid night's sleep."

Before I could respond, he shut the door, and the lock clicked into place. His footsteps were muffled as he walked slowly away. With each step, the weight in my chest grew heavier. I put a hand over my heart to ease the discomfort.

"Something weird is going on," Saphira murmured, her head tilting.

I didn't understand why she was whispering. Thorn was far enough away that we couldn't hear him anymore. "I don't know what you're—"

She placed her finger in front of her lips.

I had no clue what the gesture meant in dragon. "What are you doing? Flipping me off?"

Dropping her hand, she bit her lip. "Telling you to be quiet. Is that how *you* flip people off? Because most people know what that means. It's even in the opening to *Pretty Little Liars*."

I was so confused about what shushing me had to do with a television show. "I know it means 'be quiet,' but you're a *dragon shifter*. I thought it might mean something different to you."

She shook out her arms. "We live in the same world as you. We may have dragon magic, but overall, our gestures are the same as yours."

"Good to know." At least I could rely on nonverbal communication. "I can't hear him anymore."

Motioning to the metal, she answered, "That doesn't mean he can't hear *us*. The Wolfram Dwinn is not only stronger than a dragon, but it also limits the noises we can hear while we're surrounded by it."

His reappearance after I'd told her everything about why I'd agreed to Drake's terms now made sense. He'd listened to our conversation from wherever he'd been in the cabin.

My stomach soured. There was no telling what else he might have overheard that I'd rather he not know.

I wrapped my arms around my waist. Not knowing how dragon stuff worked was getting on my last nerve. "Anything else you might want to share with me?"

"Not that I can think of." Saphira plopped down on her side of the bed and pulled the covers over her legs. "It's not like there's an instruction manual. You're the first turned dragon I've ever known."

Her words hit the mark, and I sucked in a breath. "That's fair. It's just frustrating not knowing things that every other dragon knows. I'm trying to paint a realistic picture when I haven't mastered the fundamentals yet."

Brows creasing, she popped her lips. "I'll pretend I understood your point and tell you that you'll have to think of this as a work in progress. I'll be right by your side, guiding you."

There was one thing I knew for certain: of every dragon shifter I knew, though that group was limited, I trusted her. "Okay." I had no other option, anyway.

I crawled into bed and turned my back to her, facing the window and not the door. That was for the best. If I stared at the door, I'd be willing Thorn to reappear just so I could see him again. At least, with the window, I could only see outside. "Like Thorn suggested, I should get some rest." I forced a yawn, hoping to prevent her from asking the question from earlier again.

"Fine. I'm tired, too," she grumbled and dropped her head onto the pillow.

Silence descended, and I stared at the metal wall. My reflection stared back at me. My blonde hair was drying and looked fuller than ever before, and my gray eyes were more vibrant. My normally ivory skin had a hint of olive to it, giving me a natural glow. I barely recognized myself.

Time moved slowly as I waited for fatigue to overtake me. My mind raced with everything I'd learned. Over the past few days, my life had taken a tremendous curve, and these progeny-like feelings I had for Thorn disturbed me. I shouldn't care this much about someone who'd kidnapped me.

Just when I figured sleep would never come, my eyes closed.

Loud footsteps hurried down the hallway toward the door, waking me from my slumber. My eyes popped open, and I tried to get my bearings.

This was definitely not my dorm.

The world was brighter than ever before with colors I'd never known existed reflecting off the metal wall in front of me.

The bed jostled as someone clambered to their feet.

With that, I remembered where I was and who I was with. Now the colors made sense.

I sat up to find Saphira glaring at the door.

A key slid into the lock, followed by a *click* and the door opening. The scent of bacon wafted into the room, but that wasn't what made my heart stop.

Thorn's tall, rugged body came into view, stealing my breath. His full lips were pressed in a line, and his hair hung in his face, making him look like the *perfect* supermodel. He deserved to be painted so the memory of him would last forever and not just in my mind.

"We have a problem," he said gruffly. "A police car is on its way here."

I blinked. "Did Drake find us?"

He shook his head. "I left last night because my perimeter alert system went off. I drove away so I wouldn't alarm whoever was near the cabin, then scouted the area. I found squirrel hunters out there. When I returned, I saw that you'd escaped. I can only assume that one of them saw me carrying you and called the authorities. The monitor I have on the driveway just went off, and I was able to catch the vehicle on camera."

My heart pounded. This might be the way out of this horrible situation.

Saphira snorted. "They'll want to check the house,

and you don't want them to find Everly and me locked in a room."

He frowned. "Yes."

An engine grew louder. I turned to the window and saw the police car about five hundred feet away. The officer would be here momentarily.

She beamed. "So you're letting us out?"

"Yes, I have to." He exhaled, and his jaw twitched. "I'm going to tell you something, and all I can do is ask you not to say anything to give us away. I took you to save my parents. I have no intention of harming either of you, or I would've done so by now. I promise when the police leave, I will tell you *everything*, including how I changed Everly into a dragon." Face lined with worry, he moved to the side and gestured for us to leave our prison cell.

I blinked several times as I stared at him, my breath catching. *His parents*. That's what this was all about?

I *needed* answers.

And I needed to understand why his parents were in danger and how he'd turned me into *this*.

Saphira nodded toward the door, telling me to go first. I stood and marched past Thorn and out the door. I had to use every ounce of self-control not to brush my arm against his body. I was jonesing for the electricity that pulsed between us, desperate for my next fix.

But Saphira was watching me, and I didn't want her to ask questions I couldn't answer.

I scurried down the hall with Saphira on my heels.

Boots scuffed the ground outside, and I realized there were two officers. They wouldn't come without backup to check a threat.

As we entered the living room, my gaze followed my nose to the kitchen, which was wide open to the living room. I hadn't noticed much about it before because I'd been focused on escaping.

A rectangular table sat in the middle of the kitchen, which had black counters on top of white cabinets against one wall with a sink and a dishwasher, and the stove against the wall that faced the front of the house. Bacon and eggs were piled onto two pans on top of the stove.

My stomach growled as intense hunger swamped me.

A loud knock sounded on the door, and Saphira and I glanced at each other as Thorn tensed.

He sighed as he walked to the front door then turned around and glanced at us again. He murmured, "Please."

When neither she nor I responded, he turned around and opened the door.

CHAPTER FOURTEEN

I WASN'T sure what to do. Part of me wanted to proclaim I needed help while an equally large part wanted to remain quiet. I had no doubt that Thorn had answers. Was getting them worth the risk of remaining his prisoner? I wasn't sure.

In the doorway, two men in black police uniforms towered with their hands near their holsters.

The taller officer stood on the right, his dark eyes searching the inside of the cabin. His raven hair was cut short, and his sideburns bled into an obsidian, short-trimmed beard. His dark skin wrinkled around his eyes from constant tensing. "Good morning. Sorry to bother you, but we're checking out the area."

The chestnut eyes of the shorter officer homed in on the two of us where we stood behind the couch. His brown skin was lighter than his friend's, and his face was a little rounder, lending him a more friendly countenance. However, his jaw was set as his gaze swung between us and Thorn.

"Of course, Officer." Thorn gestured for them to step inside. "We were about to sit down and have breakfast."

Saphira took an eager step toward them, and my dragon roared and brushed my mind. I moved so our shoulders bumped, and her gaze landed on me. Her brows furrowed, and I shook my head.

The shorter officer strolled over to us, and I swallowed hard. He might have noticed our interaction.

"We had a call late last night from some hunters who saw a girl running through the woods. They then said that a man carried her back toward where she'd run from," the taller officer said as he stepped farther inside. "Your cabin is the closest to the incident, so we thought we'd check in and make sure nothing was amiss."

Thorn had been right in his assumption about the hunters. At least there were still good people in the world who called in something concerning. Not everyone would've done that.

"One mentioned it looked like the girl had blonde hair." The shorter officer studied me.

With the six years of practice at keeping my face neutral around Peter, my expression remained indifferent.

"I, for one, am glad you're here," Saphira started and lifted her chin.

Without thought, I interjected, "It was me. I was the girl out there."

Thorn closed his eyes and hung his head, which pulled at my heart.

"Thank gods. For a minute, I thought you'd lost your mind." Saphira sighed and leaned back against the back of the couch.

The taller officer reached for his handcuffs, and my stomach dropped.

I couldn't rat Thorn out. I *needed* answers. "I got restless being cooped up all day, and I went for a run."

"Everly." Saphira's jaw dropped. "What are you *doing*?"

I couldn't fault her. I probably wasn't being smart, but I was going with my gut. And my gut said I needed to hear what Thorn had to say. I believed that he wouldn't hurt either Saphira or me. "I *know*." I rolled my eyes and cringed. "I can't believe I'm telling them this, either. It wasn't my finest moment."

"You're telling us you went running into the middle of the forest in the dark while it was pouring rain?" the shorter officer asked slowly and squinted.

Thorn lifted his head, a strange expression on his face.

"Like I said, it wasn't my finest moment." I forced a laugh and twirled a piece of hair around my finger. "I worked at a vet's office a few years ago, and I learned that rain makes it safe to explore the woods if you're going to do it. Critters don't like being out in it any more than humans do, so I figured, why not?" I shrugged, hating how dumb I sounded.

Clearing his throat, the taller officer moved his hands back to his sides. "You do realize that...um...dangerous *critters* can still be out there. Bears roam these parts."

He had me there, but in fairness, I had been running for my life. I hadn't been sure at that point that Thorn wouldn't hurt us. I bobbed my head. "I had bear spray, and those critters are so big that I *totally* would've heard one." If there was an afterlife, I hoped Mom was *not* watching me now. I was certain she would not be proud of me.

All four of them blinked at me like they couldn't believe what they were hearing. Yeah, me, neither. But I was already in deep, so I continued to tread water.

"Okay, but that doesn't account for you being hauled back here by a man." The shorter officer scratched his head.

I could imagine what he was thinking, and it was probably best I didn't know for sure. "I got myself into a wee little pickle." I lifted my fingers and held my thumb and pointer finger close together. "I got lost, and fortunately, I found a spot where there was a bar of service and sent Thorn a text, informing him I was near a waterfall."

"I know the area well and had a good guess where I could find her," Thorn added, placing his hands into his jeans pockets.

"Did you, now?" Saphira pursed her lips, not helping the situation.

I sauntered over to Thorn, looping my arm through his. I almost gasped at the spark from his skin. "Ignore her. She doesn't approve of our relationship, but she's my best friend, so I brought her along."

Thorn forced a smile and wrapped an arm around me. Wanting to sell the story, I stood on my tiptoes and pecked his lips. The jolt made me gasp and grow lightheaded. I sagged into his side, the electricity strengthening between us.

"What the *hell*!" Saphira snarled.

"See." I gestured at her. "Anyway," I said flippantly and nuzzled into his side. I wanted to sneak another kiss and rub against him like a cat. Yeah, maybe I shouldn't have tried to pull off the act so convincingly. "When he found me, I thought he was a big bear and ran. I slipped and tumbled down an incline. I hurt myself, and he had to carry me home."

"That's an interesting story." The shorter officer swung his attention to Saphira. "Do you have anything you'd like to add?"

Mouth drying, I held my breath. I'd tried, but I couldn't force Saphira to remain quiet. If she wanted to tell them the truth, I couldn't do a damn thing about it.

Saphira exhaled and glanced at me, then Thorn. "I wish there were, but how could I top that?" she asked through a frown.

I released the breath I'd been holding, and Thorn's arm relaxed around me.

The two officers glanced at each other, then back to Saphira and me. The taller one asked, "You two aren't in trouble?"

"No more than usual." I beamed. That was true. Being held captive here was the same as being forced to be around my stepdad regularly.

"Well, all right." The shorter one removed a wallet and pulled out two cards. He handed one to Saphira and one to me. "If anything changes, this is how you can get ahold of us."

I examined the card, making sure they saw me take note of it. "Thank you so much. We sure will."

The two officers turned and headed to the door.

Saphira glared at me and mouthed, *We should tell them*.

I shook my head and replied, *I need answers*.

She looked at the ceiling but didn't say another word.

When the officers got to the door, they turned around

and looked at Saphira and me again. I smiled widely and waved, hoping to come off as carefree.

The taller one nodded. "Thanks for your time."

"No problem," Thorn replied as he headed to the door. "Let us know if you need anything else."

"Will do," the shorter officer said, and the two of them walked to the police car.

When the door shut, I heard the taller one grumble, "That girl's not smart."

"But she's pretty, so at least the guy's got that going for him," the other officer replied.

The three of us remained silent until the car engine started.

Then Saphira growled, "I hope we don't regret that."

I couldn't blame her. I hoped we didn't, either, especially since I was the one who had ultimately made the call.

Thorn's attention was locked on me, his jaw slack. He murmured, "Thank you. I didn't expect you to do that."

His surprise settled hard in my stomach, and I slumped. He must not be used to people protecting him.

I couldn't allow him to see how his reaction affected me. "I didn't do it for you." That was a lie. I partly had, but I controlled my breathing, hoping he didn't pick up on it. "I just want answers."

"That's fair." He chewed on his bottom lip. "And I promised them. Where should I begin?"

"At the beginning." Saphira straightened her shoulders. "After what we just did, I want to know *everything,* including how you changed Everly into a dragon. I only played along to get answers."

"Then I'll start with the king betraying me many years ago." Thorn's face hardened, and his lips curled as if he'd tasted something awful. "That's what set everything into motion."

"Impossible. I've *never* seen you before." Saphira glowered. "You haven't been in this area before, or everyone would know. You must be part of a local thunder indirectly tied to the king. That means there's no way you've been around him enough to judge whether he's a just man. One of your own leaders likely did something wrong and blamed the king."

"You're right. I am part of a small thunder." Thorn rolled his shoulders and moved into the kitchen. "One that's made up of just Mom, Dad, and me."

It was as if they were speaking a different language. "What's a thunder?" I asked.

Thorn looked at me, the angry lines smoothing into his normal, kind face. "It's what a group of dragons who live close to one another and regularly interact is called."

"So...I don't have a thunder." That figured. I'd been a loner for a long time, so why should it change now? My heart panged with loneliness, but I pushed the annoying twinge away. It was better not to count on anyone but myself. I had to remember that.

"No." Saphira smiled sadly and touched my shoulder. "But if you follow through and give yourself to Drake, you'll automatically become part of one of the largest thunders in the world."

Thorn's neck corded, and he clenched his hands. "If you want to be part of a thunder that forces people into servitude and tortures, kills, and kidnaps people, it's a great group to join."

I snorted, then clasped my hands over my mouth. I couldn't get over the irony of what he'd said. "Really?

You're bringing kidnapping into this? Isn't that the pot calling the kettle black?"

Saphira smirked. "She has a point. You're criticizing Drake for the very thing you're guilty of. And don't play dumb. We've been living in a room lined with Wolfram Dwiin so we can't escape."

"Don't compare me to *him*." Thorn pounded his chest. "I'm not forcing either of you to have sex with me so you'll give me an heir. I'm not getting *any* pleasure out of this."

There was the opening again, and I had to take it. "Then why did you kidnap us? What in the world could Saphira and I possibly get for you?"

"The answer to that proves how little either of you knows about your *king* and *prince*." Thorn pointed at the window in front of the table, but I saw nothing out of the ordinary. "It's more about you, Everly, than Saphira." He looked at her. "I'm sorry you were collateral damage, though having you both will be more effective. In Drake's mind, someone has made him look weak by taking what he considers his property. It will drive him slowly insane, and I will use his insecurity to save the two people who mean the world to me."

My mouth went dry. I hated to admit it, but his plan might work. Drake had treated me like an object, and although I wasn't irreplaceable, someone had stolen me from his guards.

Saphira lifted her hands. "That may be true about Drake, but the king is a *good* man. He wouldn't harm anyone who didn't deserve it."

"And you have no doubt about that?" He bared his teeth and clenched his hands. "That he wouldn't have marked a young boy and his nanny for death?"

She went still and swallowed, remaining silent.

That was a very specific comment. A shiver ran through me as the silence stretched.

"I don't doubt that something horrible happened to the people you love," Saphira said slowly, weighing each word. "Otherwise, I believe you wouldn't have done this. You haven't deliberately hurt us, and you have provided us with certain comforts. *Something* drove you to kidnap us."

Some weight lifted off my shoulders. I wasn't alone in those types of thoughts. His attitude went back and forth like a yo-yo, but I was beginning to realize there was far more to his story than we knew.

"I think someone is using the king's name to justify their own actions," she continued.

"I know every person involved." Thorn stared off into space. "The blame isn't misplaced."

I wondered where his mind was at that moment. With his narrowed eyes, it was as if he were seeing a different world. I took a step toward him, the electricity increasing between us, but he didn't move.

I whispered, "What happened?"

CHAPTER FIFTEEN

HIS SHOULDERS BOWED AS if carrying a heavy burden.

I had to stop myself from rushing over to help him carry it. He probably wouldn't appreciate the support, and Saphira would lose her mind. Most importantly, it wasn't my place...even if I wanted it to be.

"Any *day* now," Saphira sniped as she strolled toward the kitchen and grabbed a handful of bacon. "Unless this is your way of trying to get out of *telling* us something."

If she would just stop and watch with an open mind, she would see that whatever he had to say was difficult for him. I wanted to chastise her, but that would only delay us in getting answers.

She popped a piece of bacon into her mouth, and for the life of me, I didn't understand how she could eat at a time like this.

"Just...give me a minute to gather my thoughts," he rasped and crossed his arms.

I smiled sadly at him. "Take your time. We're not going anywhere."

"We could've," Saphira grumbled. "But you made it clear that you want to stay here, and I stupidly went along." She took another bite of bacon. "At least I'm getting to eat. That's a silver lining."

My stomach grumbled, and my mouth watered. I'd questioned her for eating at a time like this, and now I wanted to do the same thing. Eating *would* be better than scolding her...or that was my justification.

I hurried over and grabbed a piece of bacon. When I took a bite, the taste exploded on my tongue. It was better than it had been when I was human, the salt and grease like an orgasm in my mouth.

Saphira and I chowed down, waiting for Thorn to start.

After what felt like hours, he finally spoke. "A young, beautiful nanny took the six-year-old boy in her charge for an early morning walk." His tone softened, and a faint smile spread across his face. "She told him he didn't have time for breakfast, or they might miss the elk in the area."

Warmth exploded in my heart. I loved watching the elk in the mornings or late evenings. Mom would take me with her on hikes in the woods, and I would go begrudgingly. Even though I loved painting nature, I wasn't fond of actually being out in it. But for the longest time, I was the only person she had to go hiking with. To make her happy, I'd swallow my complaints because she'd sacrificed so much for me. The few times we'd stumbled upon the elk in the woods had been magical, making the miserable experience more than worth it.

"You see, the boy *loved* seeing the elk and the deer in nature. Whenever it happened, it was the highlight of his day, so he followed his nanny dutifully." He leaned his back against the wall without missing a beat in the story.

"They took in the cool morning, enjoying the breeze on their warm skin. That was when they heard a rustling in the woods nearby."

He licked his lips as the corners of his mouth dipped. "At first, the boy thought the sounds were an elk or a deer, but the nanny had tensed. She encouraged him to turn around, saying they should hurry back to eat breakfast."

I turned to Saphira to see her reaction. This story had to be part of what was driving Thorn to do everything that he was doing.

Saphira's brows were furrowed, but she didn't slow down on eating. I was fairly certain she could eat during a natural disaster.

My appetite had been ruined. His story had already captivated me.

"Another rustling noise sounded as they headed back, and an arrow came a few inches from hitting the boy in his calf. The nanny screamed for the boy to run as she stayed behind to protect him." His breathing picked up, and his eyes glistened. "The boy didn't want to run, but he wanted to make his nanny happy. So he took off... until he heard the sound of her body hitting the ground. She'd been hit by an arrow, one lodged deep in her back."

Heart hurting, I rubbed my chest. I couldn't imagine an innocent little boy going through this, and to hear how the nanny had loved that child...they must have had a special bond.

"When the man stepped from the woods, the boy knew it was over. That both he and his nanny would die. But the man stopped in his tracks and hurried to the woman and the boy." A cruel smile stretched across Thorn's face. "He said he hadn't signed up to kill a child."

Saphira laughed and wiped her greasy hands on her sweatpants. "Let me guess: the king sent the assassin."

"Yes." Thorn's irises darkened to cobalt. "He did."

"Why would you believe that?" Saphira rolled her eyes and leaned against the countertop next to the stove. "The assassin could've blamed anyone for that."

"He could have." Thorn shrugged and narrowed his eyes, taking a step closer to us. "But when the assassin instead hid the boy and nanny away, why did the king's guards hunt them down and try to kill all three of them?"

"That could've been for *anything*." Saphira sneered. "Why would *that* boy be so special that the king would want him dead? And you weren't there. How would you *know?*"

He lowered his head and locked on her eyes. "Because that boy was *me*, and the king fears *me*."

Her jaw dropped, and she blinked. "Wait." She jerked her head toward me and asked, "Did you say his name was Thorn?"

I nodded, and she blanched.

My pulse skyrocketed. Who *was* this man? And what had he done? By her reaction, I thought maybe we should've left with the police, but my dragon huffed as if she could hear my thoughts.

The tension and silence in the room smothered me. Saphira's eyes bulged as she stared Thorn down and whispered, "That's not possible."

Though I usually kept my head down and stayed away from others, patience was not one of my virtues. I'd had enough of waiting. Earlier, I'd swallowed my frustration because Thorn had been struggling, but with the cruel smirk on his face, my sympathy was gone. "What's not possible?" Whatever Saphira's revelation was, I needed to be in on it.

He lifted a brow and smiled smugly. "Oh, the king does fear me."

She let out a shaky breath. "What's your last name?"

"Wight." He crossed his arms and winked, watching her reaction. He stalked across the room, mirth in his eyes as he stood only a few feet from us.

As expected, that name meant nothing to me, and I wanted to slap the smug look off his face.

Saphira stepped closer to him, and I stumbled forward, ready to shove her back. I didn't like her getting too close to Thorn.

She pressed her lips together. "Is that the last name you were born with?"

What an odd question. All my aggression at her proximity left me. I stared at Thorn, trying to put the missing puzzle piece into place.

The smirk vanished from his face. "No, but I suspect you already know the answer."

"But..." She touched the base of her neck and grimaced. "He said you were attacked and there was nothing left of you to recover."

"Yet here I am." Thorn dropped his hands and stood to his full height. Pain darkened his irises. "The king isn't the man you think you know."

Every cell in my body screamed at me to wrap my arms around him. However, I wasn't foolish enough to believe *I* could comfort him. He was hands-down the sexiest man I'd ever seen, and I was certain he could have any woman he desired. Not that it mattered. He'd kidnapped me, so I didn't want to be with him, anyway. I'd *only* stayed for answers.

I cleared my throat, needing to exert some independence. I wanted to tap my foot, but I forced my legs to stay still. "Fill me in."

Saphira jerked her head my way, her bottom lip quivering. "Do you remember how I told you it's impossible for a human to be *turned* into a dragon shifter?"

"Of course I do." I threw my hands out to my sides. "It *just* happened last night."

"What I told you is true with one exception." She waved her hand at Thorn. "It can be done by a dragon shifter I was told died when he was a child."

My head hurt, and I was rather confident it wasn't because of my fall. I bit the inside of my cheek and regarded him. "You can make dragon shifters? How? And why would the king *fear* that?" Instead of using humans for breeders, they could find willing humans who wanted to become dragons. That seemed like an easy sale.

"I was born with a certain mark, and such is the burden of the curse," Thorn answered in a deep, raspy voice.

I rubbed my forehead where the pain was centered. "I know I called you a monster, but you turned me without my consent. I didn't mean to make you feel as if it was a curse."

A tender expression softened his face. "That's not why I called it that. It's truly a curse."

"Why would the king wait so long to have you killed?" Saphira shook her head. "You were six when someone tried, but you were born with the dragon mark on your back. Why not kill you right then and there?"

When he'd said *marked*, I'd thought he meant under a full moon or something that would reveal him as the cursed one. I hadn't pictured a physical mark on his body, but now I desired to see it…for educational purposes. Not because I wanted to see him shirtless.

"I believe he hoped the power would remain dormant." He spread his fingers and glared at his palms. "But when I was six, the magic appeared. The king and I were playing chase in the backyard, and when I raced after him to tag him, the magic surged inside me. I thought it was just a tickle in my belly, but when I touched him, I took his dragon from him."

I'd always been able to follow stories and lectures with ease and never struggled with comprehension. That was one reason my grades had been stellar during my four years in premed, but I couldn't wrap my mind around this information. Every time I thought I was on track with him and Saphira, I was proven wrong. "Why would the king be playing chase with you? I don't understand. Or…a human king probably wouldn't have a random boy in the backyard playing chase with him. And I thought you could *create* dragon shifters, not make a dragon shifter *human*. Did you give me the king's dragon?"

"No, you don't have the king's dragon. I gave it back to him as soon as I realized that I'd taken it from him by mistake. But the real answer to your questions is that I can do both—make humans into dragon shifters and take away a dragon shifter's magic." Thorn tugged at the hem of his shirt. "I don't know how to describe it, but when a dragon passes, their magic is released back into the world. I can pull the magic from the air and push it into a human, making them into a dragon shifter. It's a mixture of magic, so the dragon is unique to the person. The opposite happens with a dragon shifter. I pull their magic into my body, and I can hold on to it for a short moment or release it into the world, just as if the person died. I can't, however, pass someone's dragon to another. Their body isn't the same, and the magic would be altered."

Though the concept was foreign, I relished the fact I didn't have the king's magic inside me. I was fairly certain the king would kill me if that were the case. "But how is there enough magic to do that? I mean, there's what, a handful of you all?"

He huffed. "There are hundreds of thousands of us across the world, and we've existed as long as man."

I shouldn't have been surprised. I would be foolish to think these were the first dragons ever.

Saphira poked her tongue into her cheek. "But you gave the king his dragon back. Was it not fully his dragon? Because that could be why he tried to kill you."

"That's a good question and one I've always wondered about but never had a chance to ask because of, you know, the fear of *being murdered*." Thorn exhaled and raised his hands. "I immediately gave him his dragon back without any of his magic escaping my body. It was completely *his* magic. But I was able to get one answer over the past twenty-one years. He was afraid that I would take it away from him again and not give it back. And how can a king rule dragons if he's lost his own?"

My head reeled. The king's fear made sense, but it wasn't right to punish a six-year-old boy for something he hadn't meant to do. Furthermore, the boy had given him the dragon back. "Why didn't he just banish you from his house?" That would've resolved the problem without needing to kill a sweet, innocent boy.

His face scrunched as he swallowed hard. He took a deep breath, steadying himself to speak.

CHAPTER SIXTEEN

THE BACON I'd eaten churned, and the anticipation was worse than actually hearing the answers.

He exhaled and said, "That would have been impossible because I was his son. He couldn't banish me and have our people find out."

I blinked as I processed what I'd heard. I swore he'd said he was the king's son, which would make him a prince *and* Drake's brother. Drake, the very person who intended to breed me for heirs. I tried to keep the food from coming up again. "You're a prince?" I croaked.

"*Was* his son." Thorn karate-chopped the air. "I'm not anymore. I'm Vlad and Cassidy's son. *They're* my parents in every way that counts."

Two names, male and female...like the nanny and the assassin who'd saved them. "Is that who was with you in the woods that day?"

He nodded. "And I'm alive because of them. If it hadn't been for *both* of them, the king would have succeeded."

Saphira laughed. "Wait. You're saying that the man

who nearly shot you in the leg and shot your nanny is the same one you consider your *father*?"

His lips pulled back, and he spat, "Yes. Arman didn't tell him who his target was, and when he realized that he'd been sent to kill the prince—who was a child—and his nanny, he saved us. He and Cassidy also risked their lives to keep me safe and raise me. My loyalty is with *them* and no one else."

All my life, I'd reminded myself there were people out there with harder lives than mine. Even when my stepdad would suggest I shouldn't spend the holidays with my siblings, or when no one showed up for my high school graduation or awards ceremony, I'd pushed my tears away and tried to keep things in perspective. Thorn's story was exactly that: heartbreaking. His father had turned him away, but it was far worse than that. Thorn had lived every day with this curse, a reminder that the very people who should've protected him had set him up to perish. At least, for the first sixteen years of my life, I'd had my mom solidly by my side. "I'm sor—"

"No." Thorn's hands shook at his sides. "Don't. Cassidy and Vlad were the best parents I could have asked for. We don't have the same blood, but that doesn't matter."

I nodded, unable to say more. I hadn't meant to upset him, but he needed to realize that not everyone would've done that to him.

"Why show up now?" Saphira rubbed the arm that had hit the wall. "Why make your presence known if you've been in hiding for the past twenty-one years? That seems pretty stupid, if you ask me."

He planted his feet wide apart and breathed noisily. "I didn't have a choice. Believe me, I'd rather be far away from here, living a simple life. But the *king* wouldn't have it."

I rubbed my hands together, trying not to fidget. I didn't want to do anything to make him think I pitied him after I'd tried apologizing for something I'd had no influence over. However, seeing him so torn up broke what was left of my heart in two.

"A little over a month ago, Vlad and Cassidy left the city to shift." He pressed a fist to his mouth. "I couldn't go with them because I was called in to work at the last minute. They should've gotten home before me because I worked a twelve-hour shift, but when I got back, the place was empty."

Saphira put her hands on her hips. "That doesn't mean the king has them."

He continued as if she hadn't said a word. "I thought maybe they'd gone on a date or made a detour, so I called Cass's phone. Falkor answered, informing me they had her and Vlad."

For once, I knew who they were talking about. That was one of the guards who'd come with Saphira to pick me up. He was definitely not the warmest person, so Thorn's story was plausible.

When Thorn didn't continue, I asked, "What did he say?"

"If I wanted them to be freed, I had to turn myself in." Thorn's shoulders sagged.

"And you figured you'd kidnap Everly instead?" Saphira snorted, and her nose wrinkled with disgust. "What if they aren't willing to make that trade?"

Actually, that wasn't a bad idea. I couldn't fault him for trying to find a solution to save all three of them, and ultimately, I would wind up back with my intended fate —Drake.

My dragon roared inside my head and brushed my mind, causing my blood to thrum. I had no clue why she was acting this way, but I felt like I might lose control.

"I told you before—Drake will be desperate to retrieve Everly so he doesn't look weak," Thorn growled, his words barely forming.

"What in the scales is wrong with the two of you?" Saphira glanced from him to me. "It's like you're going to shift." She scoffed. "Both of you, take some calming breaths and get your act together."

She was right. If I were ever going to shift, I wanted the experience to be *my* choice. I suspected if the dragon thought she could control me, my human side would always be at her mercy, and I refused to be controlled by anyone or anything. I slowly filled my lungs, remembering all my yoga classes. Meditation had helped me get through things with my stepdad and siblings. Little had I known I was preparing myself to be a dragon shifter.

I closed my eyes and took a full, deep inhalation through my nose. As I exhaled, I opened my mouth wide and stuck out my tongue, making the encouraged *ha* sound. Even after just one round, the thrumming eased, and the dragon's roar quieted. I repeated the breathing technique a few more times. When I opened my eyes, I found Thorn and Saphira staring at me strangely.

"Were you coughing up a hairball?" Saphira waved her hand up and down at me. She looked at Thorn. "Maybe your magic got confused and turned her into a cat instead of a dragon."

"No, I didn't have a *hairball*." I scratched my head. "It's the lion's breath breathing technique used in yoga."

"Oh, dear gods." Saphira pinched the bridge of her nose. "This girl is definitely human."

Was she seriously judging me? I swirled a finger at her. "It got my dragon under control, which is what you wanted, so *you're welcome*."

"Can we get back to the matter at hand?" Thorn grumbled. "Or should I put you two back in your room?"

After all this, he still planned on locking us up? Lovely. "We're fine," I said quickly. "But how did you expect to get word to the king that you have me?"

He nodded. "I've been watching the dragon net. That's how I found out about you heading to Drake's. When the guards realize the trail has gone cold, they'll post something there, which will include a way to contact them."

"What's a dragon net?" That sounded straight out of a sci-fi movie.

Saphira rolled her eyes. "It's an intranet site for all dragon-related things. It's one of the main ways the king communicates with everyone. I told Drake he shouldn't have told the entire house about Everly because it was bound to get out."

Cold realization washed through me, making my palms sweaty. "Drake wanted a human to breed with, and I'm definitely not that anymore. He may go after my sister again, and I have to protect her. No matter what." My chest seized as I hurried to Thorn. "I need you to take the dragon away from me."

Thorn's head dropped, and he winced.

There was something he wasn't telling me.

I waited for a second, but he remained quiet. The urge to scream nearly took over, but it didn't compare to my dragon inside. She roared, but this time, she didn't try to overtake my senses. I knew that her reaction was more personal—she was pissed at me. She must not have been overjoyed with me asking Thorn to remove her.

"*Now* you decide to be quiet." Saphira blew a raspberry. "Unbelievable. You wouldn't shut up a second ago, but Everly asks you a question, and suddenly, that cat has your tongue."

Shaking my head, I cut my attention toward her. "Another cat cliche? Really? I'm beginning to think you have a thing against cats."

"Gross." She scrunched her face. "I love kittens and actual cats. There are cat shifters in the world, but not in the U.S. Thank gods. Those I don't like. A lion, jaguar, or cheetah is definitely not cute and way too predatory for my liking—not that I would have an issue taking them on. I'm a dragon, after all. But a true kitty cat—I'm a huge fan and have two waiting for me back home."

A dragon with pets. That surprised me, but maybe her human side liked the companionship. Because I was certain her dragon would prefer to eat them. "I didn't see you as a cat lady."

"Well, you clearly aren't good at reading people." She shrugged. "You did agree to be a dragon shifter's human breeder."

I flinched. She had a point there. "Yeah, but it's not like I thought he was a good person or..." I trailed off. This wasn't helping my case.

Thorn emanated a deep, threatening growl. It diverted my attention back to the man I needed an answer from.

My heart leapt into my throat, but I forced myself not to cower in fear like before. After all, he *needed* me. He wouldn't risk killing me, or he would've let me die at the base of the cliff. "Seriously, I need you to remove the dragon you put in me. I can't risk him going after my sister. I promised my mom I would protect her."

His growl disappeared, and he rubbed his hands together. "I...I don't know how."

Head tilting back, I lifted my chin. "That's not funny." He'd told Saphira and me that he'd taken the king's dragon from him and given it back. He'd also *changed* me.

He rubbed a hand down his face. "I seriously don't know how to do it."

"Not to state the obvious, but neither Everly nor I is buying that." Saphira tapped her foot.

"I don't blame you, but every time I've used the curse, I haven't *meant* to." Thorn stared at his palms as if they held all the answers. "With Arman, it was a tickle when I tagged him. My heart was pounding, and as soon as I saw his expression and felt something strange inside me, I panicked and gave it back to him. With Everly, I was checking her injuries and trying to calm her, even though I was scared she was going to die. The process was so fast that I didn't notice what I had done until her red-berries-and-pear scent changed to include a faint trace of brimstone."

Shit. If he didn't know how to remove the dragon inside me, I wasn't sure what to do. I guessed I would hand myself over to Drake and hope and pray he wouldn't go after my sister. That was the only option I had. "Can't you figure it out?" I wasn't above begging.

He blew out a breath. "I can try, but I'll need time."

That was fair. However, I wasn't sure how someone went about figuring out how to make magic work. "I'm not going anywhere anytime soon, and I kinda need you to remove it. Seems like you have the perfect person to work with."

Dark circles were beginning to appear under his eyes, and I'd bet it wasn't from a restless night. It had to be from the emotional trauma of the story he'd shared with us. I could see the toll his past had taken on him, and I wished I could soothe the pain.

I believed that a person's situation informed their decisions, and not necessarily how they were raised. That view always garnered harsh criticism, but it was clear that the critics lived in a more cookie-cutter world than I did. I blended in to avoid my stepdad's cruelty, not because Mom hadn't raised me to be strong and independent. I'd done what I'd had to do to survive two years under his roof until I turned eighteen. After that, I'd conformed so I could visit my brother and sister. I'd molded myself into what I needed to be to fulfill my promise to Mom.

Thorn was another perfect example. He'd been traumatized, forced into hiding, and raised by two people who had chosen to take care of him. They'd blended in with humans for over two decades, only for the king to capture his mom and dad. He was doing the only thing he could to protect them, including capturing me.

Though I didn't agree with his choices, I couldn't fault him. He was fighting for his family.

My heart ached, and I desperately wanted to throw myself into his arms. Even after everything he'd done to me, my attraction to him kept intensifying. I hated that I'd give anything to know the taste of his lips or how his breath felt against my neck. As my body warmed, I knew I had to get it under control. "Maybe you should take a nap. We can try after you wake up."

"A nap?" He gestured at the eggs and bacon. "It's morning."

Saphira spun back around and grabbed a plate next to the stove. "It's fine. You can sleep. I'm sure I can take care of this."

A cell phone rang, and my eyes zeroed in on the one sitting on the kitchen table. I hadn't noticed it until now.

Snatching it from the table, Thorn scowled. "It's Falkor."

I swallowed hard. "I...I thought you killed him." I'd seen the guards' bodies fall from the sky and land hard in the woods that day Thorn had captured us. It was crazy to think that was only two days ago.

He flinched. "I knocked them out. I couldn't bring myself to kill them."

I was fairly certain I'd hurt his feelings, but what was I supposed to think?

The last remaining restraints around my heart shattered. My gut said he was a good man, and he was finally showing me that he was. Most people would've killed the guards who'd captured their parents. If it had been Mom, I might not have been so kind.

"Maybe he's calling to see how you're doing?" Saphira suggested, though the joke fell flat.

Not bothering to address her, I shook my head. "Don't answer it."

"I have to. It could be about my parents." He swiped the phone and held it to his ear. "Hello?"

CHAPTER SEVENTEEN

JUST AS WE were making headway with Thorn, the dragon guard had to call. I wanted to growl in frustration, but I understood that Thorn had to take it. If they'd had my family, I'd have done the same thing.

Thorn paced in front of the couch, though his attention stayed firmly locked on us.

"So...it took me a few days to recover and connect the dots," Falkor said hatefully on the other end of the line. "Just as the king predicted, you grew into the exact thing he *knew* you'd become. Someone who would attack your own kind instead of handing yourself over."

I gripped the edge of the countertop, surprised I could hear the guard so clearly.

"I'll bring you Ev—er—*the girl* in exchange for Cassidy and Vlad." He grimaced and cleared his throat. "It'll need to be a place I name, and our meet-up will need to be within an hour of receiving the location."

My dragon roared inside my head so loudly that I wanted to cover my ears. Between the noise and the sharp sting ripping through my chest, my knees buckled. I had no idea what had caused this reaction. I knew I had to go to Drake. Maybe it was because I wasn't human anymore and I feared what Drake would do if I showed up as a dragon. But there was something else—I didn't want to leave Thorn.

I pushed those feelings aside. That part *didn't* matter.

"That's not how this works." Falkor chuckled darkly. "You forget you are no longer viewed as a prince, and your demands mean *nothing*. You're the *enemy*. Now let me explain how this will happen."

Thorn's pupils elongated, and he bared his teeth. "I have *your prince's* breeder. You don't get to make the demands here."

"And we have your *parents*," Falkor spat.

"So we're on even ground." Thorn's free hand fisted at his side.

Falkor snorted. "Sure. But here's the thing: Drake can find another human. She was convenient, but not the be-all and end-all. Can you say the same about your parents?"

My head sagged as terror squeezed my chest. His words validated my worst fear. I had no doubt the next human Drake "found" would be Eva. I *couldn't* allow that.

Thorn's nostrils flared. "That's not true. The king doesn't realize that Drake wouldn't—"

"If you don't turn yourself in and bring the girl with you, we'll kill your parents," Falkor interjected. "It's that simple. We'll start with Vlad since he's the traitor who didn't finish the job."

Thorn growled, his irises glowing. My dragon purred, and I understood his dragon was peeking through.

"What the crap?" Saphira stomped and pouted. "What am I? Chopped liver?"

"If you harm either of them, you will *all* regret it." Thorn's chest heaved.

I patted Saphira's arm while remaining focused on the conversation.

Falkor laughed abruptly. "Please. You can't do anything. We'll shoot you before you can get close enough. You have until noon Saturday, and if you and the girl aren't at the place in the woods where Vlad attacked you, Vlad will die." There was a quiet click, and the line disconnected.

The house fell silent.

After a long pause, Saphira sniffed. "Seriously, they didn't even ask if I was with you. They know I haven't come home. How can they be that heartless? I grew up with them."

Thorn tossed the phone onto the couch. "I told you they aren't who you think they are. And you thought I was the liar."

I hated that we were all struggling. I understood feeling unimportant and abandoned. I'd felt like that every day for the past six years. It was one reason I hadn't stayed behind to attend my college graduation. No one had been there for my high school graduation, and I hadn't wanted to live through that again. If someone had threatened Mom's life like that when she'd been alive, I would have been falling apart. It proved how strong Thorn was.

Also, the phone call had backed up his story. Even Saphira couldn't question it. The king had tried to kill him, and the very guard who'd escorted Saphira and me had just confirmed it.

She stumbled to the wooden table and sat in one of the matching wooden spindle chairs, placing her elbows on the table, and sank her head into her hands.

"You can't turn yourself in." I lifted my hands and stared at him. "You'll die if you do."

"If I don't, my parents will die." He ran his hands through his hair, pushing his shaggy bangs back. "I couldn't live with that."

I swallowed. I didn't know why it was so damn important to me, but the thought of him handing himself over made me want to kill someone. If he didn't see reason, I'd find a way to lock him up in the dragon-proof room.

"There has to be another way," I said as I walked past Saphira into the living room and stopped a few feet in front of him. "If you hand yourself over to Falkor and they release your parents, your parents will come back for you, especially if they think the king will kill you. Either way, I have to be handed over, and I need to be human when that happens."

He huffed and tipped his head back. "You're right. I have a little over two days to figure out how to make this work." He gestured to the hallway. "You two need to go back to your room."

"What?" Saphira slapped her hands on the table. "You're going to lock us up?"

"I need to leave." He winced but stood tall. "And I don't trust you two enough to leave you loose in here while I'm gone. As you can see, trust doesn't come easily to me."

"I can help." Saphira stood and leaned over the table. "My uncle is close with my dad, but he lives about fifty miles away from the mansion at the edge of dragon territory. He isn't a fan of Drake and is lukewarm toward the king. I bet I can explain the situation and get him to help. I'll ask him to find out where they're keeping your parents."

This was new information. With Saphira so convinced the king was a good man, I found the fact that her uncle wasn't a fan shocking. "Why isn't he a fan, especially if your dad is the king's advisor?"

"It's my cousin." Saphira bit her bottom lip. "He got into a fight with Drake about five years ago. He was thirteen, and it was about me. Drake had said that my opinion didn't matter and the only thing I was good for was breeding. We were in the garden behind the château while my uncle, Dad, and the king were meeting inside to discuss a situation outside of Atlanta.

"Drake told Tyson to mind his business, but Tyson told him I was smart and deserved respect. Drake shifted and attacked him. Tyson shifted, too, to defend himself. Striking hard and fast, Drake clawed deep into Tyson's back at the base of one wing. Tyson never fully recovered, and Drake told the king that Tyson had been disrespectful, but Drake hadn't meant to hurt him. I'd seen what really happened, but when I tried to speak up, Tyson cut me off, and the king fired my uncle as his financial advisor and evicted them from the home provided for the king's advisors. That's why they live on the outskirts of dragon territory. My uncle knows the truth and resents the king for believing his bratty son, and Drake for harming Tyson on purpose."

Her cousin had protected her the only way he could. He'd protected her dignity, and then he'd kept her from being another target.

"That's a horrible story, and I believe every word, but

I don't want to make your relatives a target again." Thorn's face softened. "They've gone through enough."

He wasn't accepting her help, and that was frustrating. I understood that he felt like he was alone, but we should rely on one another. "What are you going to do? Besides trying to change me back into a human?"

"I...don't know. But sitting here isn't an option." He placed his hands behind his head, his shirt inching up and showing off a small section of his stomach.

Drool puddled in my mouth, and something flamed inside me.

"The king and Drake don't have to know my uncle helped you." Saphira marched around the table and placed her hands on the back of the sofa. "Once we know where your parents are, we can plan a way to free them. I can think of a few places where they might be so the servants don't know. If it's one of those locations, I can say you beat it out of me."

His pulse thudded in his neck. "Why don't you just call him? I can't risk you leaving and not coming back, or bringing warriors with you."

"Please." She rolled her eyes. "First off, he needs to see me so he can tell I'm not under duress and legitimize your claims. And Everly would stay here with you. Do you know what Drake would do to me if I came back without her? He'd know that I left her, and that wouldn't sit well with him; he's not even negotiating for my return. Besides, I like Everly, and you need to turn her back into a human before he finds her. If I don't come back, I'll have no way of knowing if she's human again."

"Okay, then you'll tell him our location." Thorn shook his head. "I can't risk it."

I understood his hesitation—he had kidnapped us and

held us prisoner—but I figured it wouldn't hurt to put in my two cents. "What choice do you have? If she betrays you, they'll find us, and your parents could die. You're the one they want. If you let her go and she follows through, you might be able to save your family without turning yourself in."

Thorn's face flushed. "Why the hell couldn't they just leave us alone? We were hiding away from all the dragons. We were completely immersed in human life. The only exception was needing to shift once a week, but we kept the time short and sweet. We were trying to stay invisible."

"I promise I won't tell anyone this location." Saphira placed a hand on her heart. "I will come back here alone and give you whatever information I can."

I'd always heard that when someone lied, there were physical signs: increased heart rate, sweating, and an inability to maintain eye contact. Her heartbeat was steady, her skin maintained its same gorgeous complexion, and her attention was locked on him.

I had to say something. "I believe her."

He exhaled and pinched the bridge of his nose. "Fine. Go. I just hope this doesn't bite me in the tail."

"It won't." Saphira rubbed her hands together. "I'll go now so we'll have time to plan tonight. But first, I need to know where we are."

"The dragon lands are fifty miles north of here." Thorn rocked on his feet. "You can't miss it."

"All right. I'll go into the woods and shift." She headed to the front door, eager to leave.

I was certain that made Thorn more anxious, but we'd been locked in here against our will, and she was antsy to get out of the cabin.

Thorn nodded. "Remember, there are hunters in the woods, so be careful. The cops already came here to ensure Everly was okay. We don't need someone else calling about dragons."

She winked. "On it. This isn't my first rodeo." She opened the door.

"Wait," I called out. I hurried to her and pulled her into a hug. "You're also risking yourself by doing this. I don't want you to get hurt, either."

At first, she tensed, but then she returned the embrace with vigor. "Thank you. You've only known me a few days, and you already care about me more than the royals do. I'll be careful, and we'll find a way to get you out of this commitment with Drake."

"As long as we don't put my sister at risk." We had to figure out a way to free both of us from the narcissistic asshole.

She pulled back and smiled sadly. "Got it. I'd better go."

This time, I didn't stop her and watched her walk off the front porch and hurry across the driveway into the woods on the other side. The door shut before she broke through the tree line.

A low rattle sounded from behind me, and the back of my neck tingled. I spun around to find Thorn with his eyes closed, his chest shaking.

Something was wrong.

I hurried toward him as a lump formed in my throat. If something happened to him, I wouldn't know how to help him. Then his eyes opened and locked on me, stopping me in my tracks.

The air between us sizzled with electricity. Maybe Saphira shouldn't have left because now we were alone.

Though I believed he was a good guy, he hadn't been honest with me. That wasn't something I could just forgive and pretend never happened.

"What's wrong?" I asked, focusing on the agony that had been there just moments ago.

He snarled, "You can't go to him. You won't have a life. He'll never let you go, even if he decides he doesn't want you anymore."

I chuckled humorlessly. "You think I don't know that? But my sister just turned eighteen, and she has our brother. They're twins and have a close relationship, so he would get hurt in the crossfire as well. It's better if it's just me."

Closing the distance between us, he lowered his head and stared into my eyes. Between the energy surrounding us and his delicious scent swirling around me, the world tilted. If I hadn't known better, I would have thought he was staring into my soul. I felt raw and bare before him.

"You don't deserve this," he whispered and lowered his head toward me. "You should've never been thrust into this dangerous world."

I swallowed and licked my lips. The peck we'd shared had been mind-blowing; I wondered what a full kiss would be like.

When his lips were just millimeters from touching mine, I realized I might get the answer to the most important question in the entire world—how he tasted.

CHAPTER EIGHTEEN

BUTTERFLIES FLUTTERED in my stomach as his lips came closer to mine. This kiss would be my undoing. If a peck had felt amazing, this would rock my entire world, and I might never want to stop.

That wasn't an option.

Right when his breath hit my face, I took a step backward.

Everything inside me protested, and I almost stumbled toward him, wanting to finish what we hadn't even started. However, the risk of what he might take from me —my heart—might not be something I could survive, and I had to protect my sister.

His face scrunched, and he jerked upright. He cleared his throat and muttered, "I'm sorry."

Now I was the asshole, making him feel awkward and embarrassed. "You have nothing to apologize for. I'm giving mixed signals. It's just...I don't want to complicate things more between us when we have people we love at risk."

He shook his head, and his long bangs fell into his

eyes. "Let's not forget I kidnapped you. I'm sure that's part of the equation as well."

My face burned, but I lifted my chin, refusing to appear guilty. It was an excellent reason not to want to kiss him, but I'd forgotten that fact momentarily. I'd seen my dormmates act foolish over guys, so I knew firsthand how lust could make anyone stupid. But I'd thought I was above that, and oh, how the mighty was eating her own words. "Well, we're allies, right? That didn't seem like a good point to bring up when we're trying to trust each other and work together."

"Then I won't bring it up again." He rubbed his hands and backed up more.

Something tugged inside me, and I almost followed him. I had to stop acting hot and cold toward him and settle for one—er, I meant choose cold.

"Maybe you should warm up some breakfast and eat before you try to change me back into a human." The few pieces of bacon I'd scarfed down had formed a lump in my stomach. Even as a human, I could eat more than that, so stress must have been getting in the way of my appetite.

He exhaled and headed toward the kitchen. "Yeah, let me grab something. Don't you want anything else? You only ate half as much as Saphira."

"I'm good." The thought of eating anything more made me certain I would hurl. I hated vomiting in general, but I'd die if I did it in front of him. "The whole situation is making me tense."

"I understand that all too well, but to figure out how to use my magic, I'll need my strength." He strolled to the eggs and what was left of the bacon—a mere five strips. He took a plate from the cabinet to the right of the stove and filled it with food, popped it in the black microwave over the stove, and started it.

Not sure what to do, I rubbed my hands down my sweatpants. Though they were comfortable, they were too long and not my normal style. I would've liked a pair of high-rise skinny jeans and a flowy top instead of these.

"I would *love* a cup of coffee." I went into the kitchen and searched for the Keurig. When my gaze landed on a traditional coffee maker, I stopped. "An old-school drip machine?" Though I'd worked in a coffee shop, I'd handled the lattes and frozen drinks, never the coffee makers, and at home and the dorms, I'd had Keurigs.

The microwave beeped, and he removed his food. He turned to me and lifted a brow. "Yeah. I'd been about to start coffee when the cops pulled up."

I wished he had. "That's cool. I can do it." I scanned the countertop and saw white filters in a bag and a container that had the label *coffee* on it. I grabbed the container and lifted the plastic lid to find ground coffee inside. Luckily, I'd watched my coworkers work the commercial version of this, so I knew what to do. I pulled open the place that held the filter in the machine and put a filter inside, but then I realized I had no clue how much coffee to put in it. "How many scoops?" I tried to sound strong and steady.

"Four, unless you don't like it as strong." He sat at the table and took a bite of his eggs. His nose wrinkled as if the food didn't taste good, but he continued to eat like he was on a mission.

Following his directions, I added the coffee to the filter and poured water into the side. I pressed start and almost cheered when the liquid came out looking normal.

There were already three sizable brown coffee mugs set to one side.

I turned to him and pressed my back against the counter as the brewing coffee filled my senses. Since it was just him and me, maybe this was my chance to ask questions I might not get answers to later on. "Your magic doesn't sound like it's necessarily a *bad* thing. By using your magic on me, you saved my life. So...why do you call it a curse?"

He finished chewing on a piece of bacon. "Well, my biological father tried to kill me over it, so we can start there."

I winced. "Fair point." I hadn't meant to pick at the scab. "But for him to react so violently, something must have influenced him to view it that way. I'm just—"

"Are you defending him?" Thorn tilted his head back, and his nostrils flared.

Asking this question hadn't been wise. He was taking it personally, and I couldn't blame him. "Of course not. You mentioned you were born with the mark of the curse. It didn't start when you accidentally stole the king's dragon. It was like your...*the king* had expected you to do something."

"You're right. I'm sorry." He licked his lip. "Being here while my parents are in danger has me reliving the very occurrence I've tried to forget."

The coffee machine sputtered, and I welcomed the distraction. I spun around, grabbed two mugs, and filled them. "I didn't mean to make this situation worse. Forget I asked."

I sat across from him and handed him a mug.

"Thank you," he said gently. "No, it's a fair question

and one you have a right to ask, especially since I changed you."

Some tension left my body. I liked getting answers. My life had enough mysteries, such as why my stepdad resented me.

He took a sip of his coffee and set it back on the table. "In the last millennium, only a handful of dragons have had this gift. No one knows why, and little is known about the first few who had the magic. The last king who did had stories written about him. His legacy lives through some of the older dragons who are still alive after his reign. He was my grandfather."

My stomach clenched. I sensed the stories weren't good.

"He died before I was born, but I learned he used the magic unabashedly." Thorn leaned back in his chair. "He created a handful of dragons for people he deemed worthy, usually because a dragon shifter had fallen in love with a human."

I didn't understand the issue. "He was allowing people in love to be together? That sounds like a good thing."

Thorn grimaced. "It was usually a human that a dragon had become obsessed with, and my grandfather turned them against their will. That's why I'm surprised the current king is okay with Drake's plan for you, but maybe he can't afford to lose his last heir." He shrugged.

If the king was letting Drake get away with something he'd been vehemently against when Thorn was young, that had to be a bitter pill for Thorn to swallow. I laid a hand on the table and forced myself not to reach for him. I wanted to comfort him.

He ran a finger along the rim of the mug. "But what

my grandfather was known for was taking people's dragons."

"Permanently?" My eyebrows rose. "Because they did something bad?"

"If disagreeing with him is a valid reason, then yes, because they did something bad." Thorn pushed his half-full plate away.

I had to be missing something. "During riots or a rebellion?" There were times in history when leaders took a firm stand to prevent a bigger problem from occurring.

"Nothing like that. People were too scared to rebel." His lips pressed into a line. "If they disagreed with him about *anything*, right down to the color of his tie, he'd remove their dragon. Most people believe his magic corrupted him because he got worse the older he became."

"He was a tyrant."

He nodded. "And since I was born with the same magic, that's what people believe I'll become."

My belly roiled. "I'm sorry." I wasn't sure what else I could say.

"It isn't your fault. I am sorry you got wrapped up in our world." He stood and gestured to the living room. "Why don't we move to the couch, and let me see if I can figure out how to undo what I did to you without permission."

I had more questions, but this was his way of moving on from the conversation, and I didn't want to push him.

I took a large sip of coffee, surprised it didn't burn my throat. One perk of being a dragon was that I could breathe fire, I guessed.

I headed to the living room, ready to entertain myself while he got his bearings.

An hour later, Thorn hadn't achieved anything. He'd been sitting right beside me, trying to connect with his magic, while I'd clasped my hands, desperate for a way not to touch him. The jolt between us stole my breath and made me dizzy, and I yearned to feel him, kiss him, and be with him.

He huffed and placed his head in his hands. "I don't know how to do this. I don't feel anything different inside me. All I can sense is my dragon."

He'd been growing more frustrated with each passing minute, and I feared he might be at his breaking point.

"Okay." I turned toward him. "When I fell and hit my head last night, did you feel anything before you touched me?"

Sitting back upright, he squinted and stared at the wall underneath the TV. "Actually, I didn't. It was when I touched you."

At least we had one piece of the puzzle solved. "So try that now." I inched toward him, eager for the distance between us to disappear.

He swallowed, and his Adam's apple bobbed. "You want me to touch you?"

The way he said it made my chest feel funny, and I tried not to take the words like a sexual innuendo. "If that worked before."

"Right." He cleared his throat.

The way he was acting awkward despite being devastatingly gorgeous made him more endearing. He could have any woman on the planet, but he wasn't arrogant in the least. That made me more attracted to him, and there was nothing I could do to stop it.

He held out his hands and paused before touching my shoulders. Electricity sprang to life between us, sizzling from my shoulders down my spine, and to my core. I gasped from the pleasure.

He dropped his hands. "Did I hurt you?"

Great. He must not have felt the same thing I had. This was all one-sided. "No, sorry. Still getting used to being part dragon."

"You may not have to be uncomfortable much longer." He smiled sadly and touched my shoulders again.

The pleasure washed through me once more, but I'd expected the sensation and stayed relaxed.

He closed his eyes, and I stared at his long lashes. Now that he wasn't looking at me, I could take in every gorgeous feature. His cheekbones were angular and his lips so full that I'd bet they were soft as a feather. Between his looks and his love for his parents, there was no doubt he would make a woman very happy someday.

I wished that woman could be me.

Something trickled into my body, a warm energy I'd never felt before. My dragon roared in my brain, and I jerked. She'd been so quiet. The magic swirled around inside me, floating within my body.

"I feel something," I whispered.

His fingers dug into my skin as he gritted out, "I know, but I can't get my magic to attach to your dragon." His brows furrowed, and more warmth flowed into me.

My dragon mixed with the magic, and my heart dropped. He was taking her from me, but I wasn't relieved like I thought I'd be. Inexplicably, I wanted her to stay. I couldn't be attached to her. She'd been part of me for less than twenty-four hours.

His hands began to shake on my shoulders, and I

focused back on him. Sweat beaded his face as he grimaced. He was trying like hell to change me back into a human, and it was taking a huge toll on him.

"Hey," I said, but he continued to funnel his magic into me.

I cupped his cheek, and his eyes flew open. His irises glowed, his pupils slitted, and my dragon stirred. Our faces were so close, and everything inside me ached for him. There was no way I could go another second without him knowing how I felt.

"I'm sorry," he murmured, but before he could say anything else, I kissed him.

He wrapped his arms around me, pulling me against him as we opened our mouths to each other. Electricity jolted between us, and his faint vanilla flavor filled my mouth, overloading my senses.

All logic escaped me, and all I could focus on was his mouth, taste, and the way his body felt against mine. Our tongues danced together, and I threaded my fingers into his shaggy hair, loving how easy it was to grab on to.

My breathing quickened, and I moved to straddle him.

Something jingled, breaking through the bubble of desire. The doorknob turned. We weren't alone.

I jerked away, trying to break us apart, but Thorn clung to me.

Saphira couldn't find us like this.

CHAPTER NINETEEN

HIS TONGUE BRUSHED MY LIPS, and my brain fried. I'd been crazy to pull away. The connection between us buzzed like a high, making the deliciousness of his touch and kiss more intoxicating.

"What the *hell*?" Saphira yelled as she slammed the cabin door behind her.

I flinched as reality crashed over me. *That* was why I'd tried to pull away.

Thorn jerked back, making my dragon whimper and my heart ache.

Feeling that way was ridiculous, especially since I'd retreated first. We'd admitted, not even a couple of hours ago, that kissing wouldn't be wise, especially since there was no future for us together.

His magic had spurred something inside me and made me lose my mind.

Saphira stomped toward us until I felt her hovering at my side.

I wanted to hang my head and avoid eye contact, but that would make this situation more uncomfortable. I'd learned the hard way that facing issues head-on helped the confrontation. Well, that and taking full responsibility, even if it wasn't your fault.

In this instance, I *was* to blame. After all, I'd kissed him this time around.

With every ounce of self-control I possessed, I turned my head toward her.

Her long, curly hair was windblown, and her brown skin glistened in a way it hadn't during the past few days while we'd been locked in the cabin. She was a vision, and again, I wondered why Drake hadn't chosen her to be his...breeder.

Then I remembered. He needed a human, which I wasn't anymore.

"It was my fault," Thorn said and lifted his chin as if ready to fight. "Our magic melded together, and I kissed her."

My chest expanded, and my attraction to him deepened, which I hadn't thought possible. He was willing to take the blame.

"So you *take* anything you want?" Saphira pointed a finger at him. "Kidnapping Everly and me, locking us up here, and now pushing yourself on her?"

There was no way I would let him do this, especially since he and Saphira had gotten on the same page before she left. "It wasn't him. It was me. He's trying to protect me from your wrath. I kissed him for the reason he said. His magic was all inside me and mixing with my dragon. I got wrapped up in the moment and lost my head."

"Seems like more than losing your damn head," Saphira snarled as her eyes widened. "I get that maybe he isn't the villain, but he *kidnapped* us and changed you into a dragon."

Normally, I would back off, but I couldn't let this go. She was attacking Thorn, and it wasn't fair. "Oh, so he should've flown up to the car door while you were driving away and asked you to roll down the window so he could plead with us to come with him? Oh, wait, he was in *dragon* form."

Thorn gave me that same strange gaze he had when the cops had been present. His brows were furrowed, but his eyes were filled with...not confusion, but adoration.

Saphira's jaw dropped. "Are you *defending* him?"

"Yes, I am. He's in a horrible situation with no good answers. A situation we're involved in. Do you think it was a good decision to get your uncle involved?" I stood and crossed my arms.

She rolled her eyes. "No, because now he's at risk. But it was the best option we had because Thorn and his parents don't deserve *this*. Besides, I want to help so I can see what the king has done. If what Thorn says is true, then the king and the prince have been abusing their powers."

"And that's the conclusion Thorn came to when he captured us." I aimed to be pragmatic. If I didn't think rationally, emotions would take over, and that would be bad. That was one reason I enjoyed medicine. It was filled with facts and diagnostics. If you kept searching, finding an answer was inevitable. Reacting emotionally often made things worse. "If he turned himself in to free his parents, they would come back for him, risking them all, so he had to find another solution...which happened to be us."

"I'm really sorry for dragging you two into this." Thorn licked his lips. "I wish I'd figured out something else instead."

Saphira's expression softened. "*Fine.* I get why you did what you did. I'd do anything for my family, too," she said begrudgingly.

Wanting her to realize something else, I added, "And he took the blame for something *I* started to save me from *this.*" I gestured at Saphira.

"That was my fault as well." Thorn smiled sadly. "I didn't stop you."

I glared at him. He was *not* helping.

"Oh, gods," Saphira growled. "No more kissing." She tilted her head at me and said, "You do plan on handing yourself over to Drake, don't you?"

Thorn's jaw clenched.

He wasn't taking this well. That might be due to his brother having so much control over everything. "Of course I am. I can't risk Eva. When I turn myself over, I'll need both of you to keep an eye on her to make sure she and my brother stay safe. I won't be able to watch over them like my mom asked me to. So far, Thorn hasn't been able to take back my dragon."

"I will." Saphira placed a hand over her heart, but then she wrinkled her nose. "Maybe it didn't work because you *attacked* him."

I scoffed and puffed out my chest. "I did not *attack* him. I ki—"

She lifted a hand. "Stop right there. We're going with attacked because I need to unsee what I walked in on. I'll have nightmares for months. I seriously thought you were eating each other."

That image was *so* not sexy. He was the first man I'd ever really kissed, so maybe I'd been horrible at it. My stomach dropped as my neck and ears grew uncomfortably hot. I was certain I'd never be able to look at Thorn again without wanting to hide.

Thorn cleared his throat. "That's not why I couldn't turn her back. I don't know how long I funneled magic into her, but I *couldn't* latch on to the dragon. Then my magic actually rejected taking her dragon from her. I pushed more into her to override it."

I'd wondered why he'd increased the amount flowing into me. I faced him again. "I thought you took the king's dragon."

"I *did*. My magic latched on to it easily, just like I gave you yours without a struggle." Thorn lifted clenched hands. "I don't know what the hell the problem is."

"Maybe you didn't try?" Saphira rocked back on her feet and leveled her gaze at him. "Keeping her a dragon is one way to stick it to Drake and thwart his plan."

She was right, but I'd *felt* everything he'd done. I insisted, "His magic swirled around my dragon. I felt him trying to connect with her, but it wasn't happening. My dragon wasn't even worried."

"Forgive me for thinking you might be biased." She cocked a brow.

"Turning her over to Drake like *this* while the king has my parents doesn't bode well for me, either." Thorn inhaled slowly and lowered his arms. "Believe me when I say I tried."

Saphira shook her head and grimaced. "You're right. I'm sorry. This whole situation would be easier if you were the bad guy."

I understood that sentiment far too well. "Did you learn anything from your uncle?"

Thorn stood and crossed his arms. He swallowed hard and remained quiet.

"No, but I didn't expect to. I told you both that." She raised her hands. "But he'll talk to Dad and get us some answers. There's a catch, though."

Thorn glanced at the door and rasped, "Did you tell them where we are?"

"What? No!" she exclaimed. "You really do have trust issues."

He bared his teeth. "When your father tries to kill you and hunts you for the rest of your life, lack of trust gets ingrained in you."

We were losing focus, and I wanted answers. "What's the catch?"

"He was hesitant to get involved and told me to stay out of it. He says going against the royals will cause me grief." Saphira wrung her hands, not looking like the confident dragon she was. "So...I told him who our kidnapper is."

"*What*?" Thorn snarled. "Why would you do that?"

"To get him to *help* us." She stomped a foot as she glared at him. "He didn't believe it. He told me to come back tonight with *you*, and he'll give us the information. He has to see that you're alive with his own eyes. Everyone believes you're dead."

Well, she was certainly blunt. I sighed. "We're aware everyone believes that, Saphira."

Thorn chuckled, and my stomach flipped. "He wants me to come to dragon lands to visit him. Really? I might as well hand myself over to the king."

I didn't know how the dragon lands were set up, but I could see why he was hesitant. If there were guards on its perimeter, they would be watching the area closely now that Thorn had Saphira and me.

"He wants to meet with you twenty miles south at a

stream where Tyson and I used to go when he wanted to get away from the thunder after his injury." She rocked on her feet. "We never saw humans there, and it's a safe location. It's deep enough in the woods that humans rarely travel there and close enough to the thunder that a rogue dragon wouldn't hang out that close to our homeland."

It did sound like a happy medium. "I understand his hesitation. He probably wants to see who Saphira has been with since she went missing."

"Are you sure he can be trusted?" Thorn scratched his neck. "Can't I call him instead?"

"I trust him, and he wants to see you. He hopes you *are* alive." Saphira closed her eyes, and her face twisted in agony. "He hates the king and Drake. I think he wants to meet you to see if you became what everyone said the curse would make you. If I know him, he's hoping you're a decent man and might want to take your place in line to the throne. Tyson gets ridiculed and barely ventures outside the house unless it's with me to go to the stream I mentioned."

Thorn leaned his head back and stared at the ceiling.

"It's up to you," I said. I understood the risks of going and the risks of remaining here. "One way, we might get answers, and the other way, we have to hope we can find where your parents are being kept. As soon as the warriors are alerted to your presence, they'll call for backup. We need to know exactly where we're heading."

"Either way could go badly." He chewed on his bottom lip and turned to me. "What do you think?"

My heart pounded. Outside of the classroom, no one ever asked for my opinion. I fidgeted and pulled my thoughts together. "I trust Saphira, and if she believes her uncle just wants to see you to confirm who you are and that he might have hope, it's worth the risk. It's not like the king isn't aware you're alive."

"Okay." He nodded. "That's what we'll do. What time are we supposed to meet him?"

Saphira smiled. "Midnight. That way, he has time to talk to Dad. Luckily, my uncle lives on the edge of dragon territory and is out of favor, so guards don't patrol there. He can sneak away." She leaned toward us over the back of the sofa. "I promise you he wouldn't betray me. We can fly in and out with no problem."

Fly.

My stomach soured. "Wait. I haven't done that before."

"You'll be fine. You'll have to learn, anyway, for your dragon to fully sync with you." She waved my concern off as if it were silly.

I tensed. "Okay, but that isn't comforting."

Thorn placed a hand on my arm. "We'll be with you the entire way. Saphira can shift with you, and I'll stay nearby in dragon form in case we run into any issues. You'll have the two of us to help you."

His words released some tension in my stomach, but my lungs struggled to work as I tried to fight my nerves. Saphira was right: I'd have to try eventually, and it would be better with them there to support me.

There was one thing that would take my mind off having to shift... "Why don't we have lunch? Is there a pizza place we can order from that delivers here?"

"You do realize we're in the mountains?" Thorn grinned at me.

"Yeah, but people still like pizza out here, right?" I didn't know how to cook, so pizza was the default when I decided to stay in. "Or we can order something else and DoorDash it."

"With how far they'd have to travel, that would be expensive." Thorn shook his head.

Apparently, I was that easy to read. "Does someone know how to make something? We always ate out or brought food in."

"And if your father is the king's advisor, you're probably as spoiled as she is," Thorn said, nodding at Saphira as he strolled into the kitchen.

Saphira stuck out her tongue. "Maybe. But I'm sure Everly and I could manage *something*."

"Leave the cooking to the experts." He pulled out a skillet. "I make a mean grilled cheese."

I smiled. At that moment, it felt like we were three friends hanging out and at ease. I just hoped that didn't change between now and when we left.

THE REST of the day passed in a blur. Saphira and I played checkers and talked fashion while Thorn watched a baseball game on TV. My competitive side leaked through every time I won a match, a vice I was well aware of. However, wanting to be the best was the main reason I was at the top of my premed class, and it had helped me get into the medical program at the school.

But my impending shift hadn't strayed far from my mind.

Thorn entered the house, his pupils elongated. "The coast is clear of humans. We can go outside and shift."

Soon enough, the three of us were walking out the front door to meet Saphira's uncle, Thorn with a large duffel bag slung over his shoulder. The importance of what we were about to do struck me, and my lungs seized. How was this my life? I hadn't even processed that I wouldn't be attending classes this summer or, more than likely, ever again. Protecting my sister was costing me not only my freedom but also my dream of helping others. In all the turmoil, I hadn't thought through everything I was giving up.

"Hey, I don't need you freaking out, too," Saphira grumbled and bumped shoulders with me.

If I'd been human, I would've fallen and skidded across the gravel driveway. Now, her mild razzing was a mere annoyance.

"Sorry, I was lost in thought." Thinking about how my entire life had changed in the blink of an eye, all because my stepdad had embezzled a million dollars from a dragon prince.

I wondered if that was why he'd been acting so strange the last few months while Mom had been alive. He'd grown cold and distant, mainly toward me, but he'd put up a barrier between himself and Mom and my half siblings as well. He'd just tolerated them better.

The moon shone down in a cloudless sky, and when I looked up, I went still with amazement. My entire human life, I'd believed the night sky was dark blue, but my dragon eyes told a different story.

The sky still appeared mainly dark blue, but there were green and yellow splotches throughout the atmosphere. Yet what made it so breathtaking was how brightly the stars shone, like beacons and spots of cobalt and pink swirls from the center of the Milky Way.

When things calmed down, I would have to paint this image for humans to see.

"Are you okay?" Thorn paused beside me and followed my gaze skyward. "Do you see something concerning?"

"I've never seen the sky like this before." I winced at my breathy tone. I probably sounded very cliché to him. "Human eyes don't see all the colors, and they're breathtaking."

"Well, you'll have the rest of your life to see the sky since Thorn can't turn you back." Saphira looped her arm with mine and dragged me toward the tree line. "Let's hurry up so we aren't late to meet my uncle."

She was right. I was dragging my feet. I glanced over my shoulder and saw Thorn's scowl before he hurried after us.

The closer it got to eleven-thirty, the more stoic he became.

Soon, we were walking into the tree line, and I stared at the surrounding red spruces and balsams, seeing patterns and colors in their branches and remaining leaves I'd never known existed.

Thorn tossed his duffel bag to the ground. "I brought clothes for us to change into once we arrive."

I nodded and swallowed hard. I'd been dreading this aspect for a while, but Saphira had sworn that my dragon would take control and the transformation would come naturally. Thorn headed deeper into the woods, and I heard noises of something large nearby—he'd already shifted into dragon form.

Saphira stripped down next to me and waved her hands, encouraging me to go on.

I inhaled shakily. "Let's see how this goes."

"Remember to allow your dragon to take over. That

will be the hardest part, but if you do that, everything else will fall into place," Saphira reminded me.

She stared at me, making my skin crawl. "Got it." I closed my eyes, not wanting to see her watching me, and searched for my dragon.

Finding her wasn't hard. She immediately brushed my mind. Forcing my body to relax, I waited.

Nothing happened.

What the hell? By being calm, I was letting her know she could take control, yet she sat there as if waiting for an invitation.

Of course I struggled with the one thing that was fundamental to being a dragon—shifting. I wasn't sure what she wanted, and we needed to go.

"Don't get upset. Just talk to her like you would a friend," Saphira murmured beside me.

Lovely. This wouldn't be awkward at all. *Please, dragon, work with me, here.*

At that, she wrapped gently around my mind, and her magic streamed through my blood. My body expanded, growing larger, and I couldn't believe it. The dragon *had* needed a freaking invitation.

I opened my eyes. Silvery scales shimmered all over me. I lifted my head, and the ground underneath me appeared farther away than usual. I regained my equilibrium, and my dragon urged me forward, tugging me around the bush to see the object of my desire.

Thorn.

Then something jolted through my heart and changed my whole world.

CHAPTER TWENTY

THORN'S SILVERY plum scales were more gorgeous through dragon eyes. I grew dizzy as I noted the moonlight reflecting off them. The silver glistened, further enhancing the purple. He was the most gorgeous creature I'd ever seen, human or dragon.

Something settled deep inside my heart, and it felt lighter as I edged toward him. Even if I'd wanted to stop, there was no way I could. I was *meant* to be beside him.

His sky blue eyes took in every inch of me, too.

The thought that my first time flying would be with him made the situation more extraordinary. I finally understood what it meant to be alive. The electricity that had shot through me in human form had been a mere taste of what it was in dragon form.

With every step closer to him, the electricity changed to something like a lightning bolt that constantly sizzled between us.

A loud huff sounded next to me, and something rammed into my side.

Saphira.

She'd shifted.

I'd expected to stumble from the pressure, but my dragon countered the momentum, and I didn't budge.

Thorn emanated a low, threatening growl.

I was certain he didn't like how she'd rammed into me, but we couldn't converse in dragon form. It was the only way she could get my attention, seeing as I'd been transfixed by Thorn.

Saphira moved in front of us, her footsteps shaking the ground. Her butterscotch scales shimmered and contrasted nicely with her mocha eyes.

I jerked my gaze back to Thorn, wondering if I'd lost his attention to her. The mere thought made my dragon angry, but my chest relaxed as he took a protective stance beside me and glared at her.

She rolled her eyes, a hint of her human side peeking through, and tilted her head skyward.

I understood what she was saying: we needed to go.

Though my hands and feet were touching the ground, my left talons rubbed what would've been my right wrist, searching for Mom's bracelet out of habit. My stomach dropped before I remembered Saphira had told me to leave it behind. I'd left it on the kitchen table where I could pick it up first thing upon our return.

I brushed my head against Thorn's long neck. I wanted to calm him, and my dragon had taken control, knowing our touch would do just that.

He huffed at her and nuzzled me back.

Butterflies took flight inside me. I was way too giddy in this form.

Saphira shifted her weight back and used her front right talons to kick at the ground.

Her show of impatience was similar to that of a horse. My dragon snarled in my head.

Great. She and I were getting along *so* well in this form.

Moving a few steps away from me, Thorn spread his wings. He flapped them slowly but didn't lift into the air.

After a second, I realized he was showing me what to do.

Though I understood the theory, I wasn't sure how fast to move them or how far to lift and lower them. What if I got high into the sky and lost momentum? I'd been so concerned with shifting that I hadn't realized I'd also have to fly.

Following his lead, I spread my wings, the sensation foreign as my back moved in a way it never had before. I raised and lowered my wings like he was showing me, but they shook from a lack of control.

Saphira stood back on all four legs and moved her wings in the same way as Thorn but faster, and she rose slowly, hovering several feet off the ground, showing me how it was done.

There was no way I'd be that graceful, but we had somewhere to be. I couldn't just stand here like an insolent child.

Taking a deep breath, I moved my wings faster, and my large body shot skyward. Tree branches smacked my face and chest, but I couldn't dodge them as I zigzagged up.

When I broke through the trees, I took a deep breath and tried to get my bearings...which was a horrible idea. My wings stopped moving as quickly, and I tumbled down.

Thorn and Saphira raced toward me, but I was

already dropping back into the tree cover. Limbs cracked, and one branch stabbed me in the side. I flipped over so I was staring into the night sky, and then I slammed into the ground, my rump taking the brunt of the impact.

Pain shot through the back of my head, and I roared as I attempted to get up. Unfortunately, I'd wedged myself between two tree trunks, my body stuck tight. I wasn't sure how the trees hadn't toppled over. I couldn't roll, and with my back aching, I wasn't strong enough to sit up.

I was trapped.

Thorn crashed through the treetops, rushing toward me. Though it was hard to tell his expression in dragon form, I could sense his emotions through his eyes—he was worried.

My dragon grumbled inside my head, angry over how silly we looked now that Thorn was here. I didn't need to hear her displeasure. I already wanted the ground to open up and swallow me whole. I'd never been athletic, and that had carried through to my shifter form.

He landed near my head and checked on me. Once he realized I wasn't seriously injured, he slid his front legs —arms?—under my shoulders.

The familiar bolt of lightning coursed between us, and I was tempted to lie there and enjoy his touch. Then Saphira appeared.

I didn't want another lecture once we got back. This time, when Thorn pushed, I tried to sit upright and got unwedged.

Soon, I was able to stand, easing the pain from my entire weight pressing onto my back.

Saphira shook her head, communicating enough for me to know that she was either appalled or found my attempt to fly hilarious. Either way, I'd never hear the end of this.

I wanted to shift to human form and tell them to go on without me, but that wasn't an option. I didn't need to give Thorn a reason to abandon the plan, and he wouldn't leave me behind.

I would have to learn to fly.

Thorn blew out a breath, his irises darkening with concern.

If I didn't do something soon, he'd shift back. Asking my dragon for help to shift earlier had worked, so I might as well try that again. I closed my eyes and thought, *Can you help me fly?*

Though I couldn't see my dragon, I could sense her inside me. She growled and brushed against my mind. My natural instinct was to not let her in, but maybe she needed that to fly.

I took a deep breath and relaxed, and her magic flooded through me. When I opened my eyes, my sight was the same, but I could sense life all around me. Before, I'd only seen and heard the woodland animals. Now I could tell that raccoons and opossums were scurrying through the underbrush as far as a few miles away, close to the stream.

My wings flapped, the motion fluid and natural. They didn't feel like a foreign part of my body but rather like they had always been there. The weight on my limbs lifted, and soon, I felt nothing underneath them. The best part was that I was no longer petrified of falling. Granted, I was only a foot off the ground, but I'd take the win.

Saphira nodded and flapped her wings, following my lead. Thorn stayed on the ground, afraid that I might fall again, which annoyed me.

Instead of waiting for him, I flew higher. We'd planned not to stay on the ground too long in dragon form to avoid detection. Even though I couldn't sense any humans nearby, I didn't want to take chances.

Saphira and I pushed our wings harder and broke through the treetops. As the cool night air brushed my scales, an exhilaration I'd never experienced before surged through me. This high in the sky, no one could touch me. Not my stepdad, not my debilitating tendency to please when it came to my family, and not even my perfectionist side where I had to be the best to prove I was worthy. I was so high up that if there was a Heaven, I had to be close to it, and I had no doubt that was exactly where my mom was.

The beat of strong wings echoed behind us, and I didn't have to look to know it was Thorn. Not just because he was the only other dragon around, but the *zing* that surged between us was growing stronger, indicating he was catching up.

Saphira pulled in front, leading us to the place where we were to meet her uncle. It was almost comical seeing her fly with the black duffel bag clutched in her talons.

I didn't rush to catch up, enjoying my current pace. I surveyed the ground, reveling in the clear night that allowed me to see everything below. Even this high—an altitude I'd been close to only on an airplane—I could make out a handful of cars spiraling down a windy two-lane road.

As Thorn caught up to me, his tantalizing scent of minty amber and brimstone filled my nose. It was the best scent in the entire world. The only thing as delicious had been his faint vanilla taste when we'd kissed.

My attention was locked on him. As a dragon, I

could tell that Thorn was as strong in this form as in his human one. I doubted there was any dragon who could rival him in strength and size. He was thirty feet tall, at least ten feet taller than my dragon. The diamond flecks in his sky blue eyes captivated me, and I tried not to focus on my fear of never seeing him again once I surrendered myself to Drake. The thought was too painful.

Saphira glanced back at us, then nodded down and to the right.

My gaze followed where she'd indicated, and I saw a stream. That had to be where we were meeting her uncle.

My body suddenly felt heavy. I didn't want this moment to end. I couldn't believe we were already at the meeting place, but at least I had the return flight to look forward to.

There were no hints of humans. The closest car was at least thirty miles away.

We began our descent, and Thorn's wings tensed and flapped more briskly. I hated the turmoil plaguing him. Not only did the king have his parents, but now he had to face someone he'd once considered one of his people.

By the stream stood a man who had to be Saphira's uncle. He watched us descend, his emerald eyes and bald head reflecting the light of the sky. He rubbed a hand over his raven goatee as the dark skin around his eyes tightened.

He didn't seem comfortable about the meeting, either, and I wondered why he'd demanded to have it.

The three of us landed half a mile away, where red spruces and balsams grew thick. We'd have cover when we shifted back into human form. As my feet touched the ground, I wanted to shoot back into the sky. But my sister's freedom was at risk, and who knew what kind of prison Thorn's parents were being held in?

Thorn glanced from side to side, getting a feel for the place. I didn't sense anything odd, but he had been a dragon much longer than I had. After a pause, he snorted and walked into the trees.

As soon as his handsome, strong tail was out of view, Saphira tossed the duffel bag in front of us.

Now *I* had to shift. That would be fun.

Beside me, Saphira's form began to shrink. She didn't struggle at all, but then she had been at this her entire life.

Last time, talking to my dragon had helped. *Can you help me shift back into human form? We need to protect our sister.*

Unhappiness coursed through me. My dragon wasn't ready to relinquish control, but I felt her separate from my mind, and when she did, my body shrank.

Back in human form, Saphira unzipped the duffel bag. "Look at you! You shifted right back without issue. Call me impressed."

When the wind blowing against my body became chillier, I glanced down to see I was back in my naked human body. "My dragon and I are starting to have an understanding."

"Good," she said as she tossed me the smaller pair of sweatpants and a shirt.

I quickly dressed, not wanting to risk her uncle searching for us and finding me like this. I slipped on some tennis shoes that were a size too big and exhaled, feeling more like myself and able to meet someone.

"Thorn! It's your turn. Everly and I will go meet my uncle," she said as she looped her arm through mine.

The ground shook as he approached us. I wanted to

hide and watch him shift, but Saphira wouldn't release her hold on me and dragged me away.

That was for the best. The last thing I needed to be was a creeper.

We walked through the tree line and found her uncle standing where he'd been when we'd flown in.

"Saphy." He smiled and placed his cell phone into his pocket. "I was beginning to wonder if you'd be here."

"Sorry. We had some strange delays." Saphira glanced at me but didn't tell him it was my fault.

Interesting.

"Where's the *supposed* prince?" Her uncle looked past us into the woods.

"He's shifting and getting dressed," she answered, and placed a hand on my shoulder. "This is Everly. Everly, this is my uncle, Brenton Asher."

Normally, I was good at meeting people, but this was the first dragon I'd met as a dragon myself, and I wasn't sure what the right greeting was. "Hi, Mr. Asher. It's nice to meet you."

"I wouldn't be so certain." He bit his bottom lip and wiped the sweat from his brow.

"What's wrong?" Saphira stood straight. "Is Tyson okay?"

"Nothing. He's fine." He cleared his throat.

A branch snapped, and that bolt of lightning shot down my back. I hadn't expected that intensity in human form, and I gasped.

Thorn's footsteps hurried, and soon, he reached my side. "Everly, what's wrong?"

I was certain I shouldn't answer that question. "Sorry, just a little overstimulated."

My feet were traitors that inched closer to him.

"Oh, dear gods," Brenton gasped and stumbled back. "It *is* you. I thought Saphira had gotten it wrong."

"Clearly, I didn't. But why are you so sure?" Saphira tilted her head.

"Even though Thorn didn't know me, I was around the castle when he was small. I saw him with his nanny often." Brenton placed a hand on his chest, looking as if he'd seen a ghost. "He's an exact mixture of the king and queen."

That was funny. Even though Thorn and Drake had similar features, I wouldn't have thought they were siblings right away. Drake's features must favor one parent.

"I've seen many people as a child, but I don't remember them." Thorn moved so our arms brushed. "Did you find out where they're keeping my parents? I need to rescue them."

"Oh." Brenton pulled at the collar of his thin white cotton shirt. "Yes. Well, I didn't quite get an answer. I tried talking to your father, Saphy, but—"

Thorn tensed beside me and looked at the sky. "We've got incoming."

CHAPTER TWENTY-ONE

JUDGING by the way Thorn's body thrummed and our proximity to dragon territory, the "incoming" wasn't a good thing.

A lump formed in my throat, and I glanced at the sky for the threat.

"I thought you said we could trust him," Thorn rasped and glared at Saphira. "Are you in on this?"

"No! Of course not." Saphira shook her head, and her brows furrowed as she gaped at her uncle. "What did you do?"

"I—" he started.

Thorn cut him off. "We don't have time for this. Everly, get out of here. I'll be right behind you."

I laughed, surprising myself, the sound maniacal even to my own ears. "You think I'm going to leave you?"

Then I sensed the presence Thorn had. The threat wasn't coming from the sky, but rather from the ground. My attention focused over Brenton's shoulders as two figures dressed in black raced toward us. One of them was Ladon, and the second was a woman.

Even with the black helmets, I could make out the edges of the woman's bleach-blonde bangs falling a little over her cinnamon-brown eyes.

The strength of my vision as a dragon shifter still unsettled me.

Ladon and the woman carried huge rifles on their shoulders, the barrels larger than normal, which looked odd.

"Yes, you'd better leave," Thorn snarled, as he lifted me by the waist and placed me behind him.

The lightning that bolted between us wasn't enough to quash my anger. These warriors were after *him*, not me. If anything, he needed to leave.

A *click* sounded behind me, and I spun around to find Falkor looking out from behind a red spruce about a hundred yards away, rifle pointed at us. He pulled the trigger.

I pivoted and tackled Thorn from behind, and he fell forward. He had about a hundred and fifty pounds on me, but he hadn't been expecting my assault and toppled like a tree.

His knees and hands hit the ground as I plastered myself over his back. Something *whoosh*ed over our heads. The bullet punched into the earth, and dirt was launched into the air.

Jerking my head up, I spotted the bullet a foot shy of hitting Brenton. Wait, that wasn't a bullet. It was a dart.

Saphira hissed, "They've got tranq guns."

I must have misunderstood her. That was something people used on *animals*.

My heart sank. That was *exactly* what we were.

My human part wanted to freeze, but my dragon appeared, forcing me to my feet. Thorn stood as well, and his jaw twitched. Just as I glanced back at Falkor, Thorn sacked me.

Unlike him, my whole front hit the ground, the overgrown grass getting stuck in my teeth. To make matters worse, he settled his entire weight on top of me. He was so heavy, I couldn't breathe. Something hit the ground close to us, and I realized he'd protected me from a dart.

That wasn't how this was going down.

I bucked underneath him, but it was like slamming into a brick house. I got that he was a dragon, but his strength should have been impossible.

My lungs screamed, and I muttered, "Can't breathe."

His full weight lifted off my body.

"If we stay much longer, they'll capture you," Saphira said from her spot beside us. "They have Jessie and Cedric with them."

I had no clue who they were, but by the way Thorn sucked in his breath, I thought he did.

"Of course they'd bring their four strongest warriors." Thorn rolled off me and glanced in both directions. "We have to run. We're sitting ducks here."

I wasn't a strategist, but his analogy fit our circumstances. "Then let's *do* that." I was an action-type person...unless I was frozen in fear. Go figure.

Not wanting to stick around to see who went first, *I* moved. But instead of running away, I figured why not run directly at the warriors? They wouldn't expect that, and they weren't targeting me.

Since Falkor was the only one shooting, I'd start with him. I pivoted toward the warrior and ran at him, hoping my path would block his easy shot at Thorn.

"Everly!" Thorn roared. "What the *fuck* are you doing?"

"I'm not a rocket scientist, but I'm pretty sure she's running toward Falkor instead of *away*," Saphira answered. "She's not thinking clearly."

Arms grabbed my waist, but the jolt was missing. Saphira's freesia smell filled my nose as she yelled, "Thorn, *go*." She tossed me toward the stream.

My body soared, the air whipping around me, but I landed on my feet. Now I was out of range of the warriors' current target.

Thorn and Saphira raced toward me. Two darts landed where they'd been a second before.

Heart pounding, I fought the urge to race toward them. That would only slow them down.

A dart whistled through the air and hit the back of Thorn's foot.

No. This couldn't be happening.

Instead of collapsing, Thorn continued to run, his speed not impacted. His nostrils flared as he pointed behind me. "Move!"

"Your foot," I spat as he and Saphira reached me.

He glanced down and paled. He reached below and yanked the dart out, and my heart began to beat again. The dart had hit the sole of his shoe. *That* we could survive.

"Thank gods," Saphira sighed.

With the immediate threat handled, I took off to the left, unsure where to head.

As I took a few steps, someone ran up behind us. I looked back to see Brenton right behind Saphira.

She clenched her hands at her sides. "What do you think—"

Thorn rushed past her and punched Brenton in the

nose. Brenton's head jerked back, and blood gushed down his mouth and chin.

Former Everly would've been appalled, but Dragon Everly knew the bastard deserved it.

The hairs on the back of my neck rose. We'd stopped for too long. Falkor, Ladon, Cedric, and Jessie were almost upon us. Knowing that Brenton was injured and would likely slow because of that, the three of us moved in sync and took off running.

"There!" Ladon yelled from our right.

They were rushing to intercept us instead of shooting.

"Saphira, you know the area. Run!" Thorn murmured urgently.

"Don't shoot unless you know you can hit Thorn," Falkor yelled. "We're low on tranqs. He's the actual threat."

At least they didn't have unlimited ammo. That was one silver lining.

Saphira took off, damn near blurring past me. Thorn gestured for me to go, and he would take up the rear.

That wasn't smart—there was no way I was even half as fast as Saphira—but I'd learned he was stubborn, so the best thing I could do was move and find a way to get behind him.

I ran as fast as I could, which was nothing to marvel at, though I moved quicker than if I'd been merely human. Maybe it would be best if I shifted into dragon form?

Saphira was almost out of sight ahead of us, but there wasn't a damn thing I could do.

"Tap into your dragon," Thorn commanded from behind me.

He made it sound simple, which it was for them, but

not for this newly turned dragon. That would be like me scoffing at him after he bought his first paint set and tried to recreate *Girl with a Pearl Earring*.

Impossible.

"This is going to be a piece of cake," Jessie said from way too close for comfort.

A shiver ran down my spine. They were going to catch us.

As if fate was real and a legit bitch, a man I'd never seen before appeared on my left, just past a balsam fir I was running by, and steamrolled me. My body lurched to the side from the impact, and the man spun me around so he was at my back and we were both facing Thorn. His hot breath hit the top of my head.

"Let her go, Cedric," Thorn commanded.

"You're not a prince anymore," Cedric seethed. "Just a criminal to bring to justice."

I snorted, wanting to draw the warrior's attention away from Thorn. "Why is he a criminal? Because he has magic you idiots don't understand?"

Cedric breathed rapidly just as Falkor walked out of the trees to Thorn. On the other side, Ladon and Jessie stood across from Falkor, their dart guns trained on Thorn.

My dragon surged and brushed against my mind. Amazingly, I understood what she was telling me. Falkor didn't have his gun raised, so he was likely out of tranqs.

In the commotion, all four of them had been focused on who they viewed as the threat.

But they weren't expecting *me*.

All right, friend, I thought to my dragon, keeping my mind open to her. *Let's have a little fun. Let's shift and protect Thorn.*

My dragon roared with excitement and melded with my mind.

Unlike the first time I'd shifted, there was no resistance. I could sense my dragon's magic flooding throughout me, indicating the shift was underway.

"What the—" Cedric gasped as his grip on me loosened.

I wasn't sure if it was because he was surprised or because my neck was expanding. It didn't matter either way.

The larger I grew, the more uncomfortable I got, as if there was something lumpy underneath me.

Ladon and Falkor stared at me, jaws slack.

My attention landed on Thorn, ready to protect him, but he'd used the distraction to rush Falkor.

The cobalt-eyed warrior heard Thorn, and his hand went for the knife sheathed at his waist.

My stomach churned with acid. I couldn't allow Thorn to get injured.

I went to rescue him, but Thorn reached Falkor and punched him in the face. Falkor swung the knife at his neck, but Thorn jerked back, and the knife missed the mark.

"I thought you said she was *human*," Jessie gasped from below. "If we'd known, maybe Cedric wouldn't have been *sat on*."

Oh, so that was the lump under my ass. I'd rather have not known that fact. Now I was very uncomfortable with both the lump and *the reason* it was there.

"She *was*," Ladon said with shock. "He must have changed her."

Since Thorn had Falkor handled, I'd focus on these two.

Something hot inched up my throat. Great, I was going to throw up in dragon form. At least I had two places to target.

Smoke trickled from my nose.

"Shit, she's gonna blow!" Ladon exclaimed. "Run! We need to stay human to use our tranqs."

The two of them turned and ran back the way they'd come as I opened my mouth and flames shot out.

I couldn't believe my eyes. The human part of me was both panicked and mesmerized, but my dragon was in full control.

Both warriors were out of harm's way, which had been my dragon's plan. Neither she nor I was a murderer. We were two parts of the same person.

Thorn had Falkor's knife and used the butt of the weapon to knock the guard in the head. Falkor dropped like a sack of potatoes, knocked out again.

Good.

I flapped my wings and glanced downward to find Cedric knocked out, too. His chest was still moving, but he wasn't a threat.

I soared upward and flew after Ladon and Jessie. They'd split and were running in opposite directions. I roared in frustration. All four warriors were trained and would be strategic.

I sensed Thorn racing after me. Instead of rushing to safety, of course his ass was coming to help me. He had to be staying in human form so he could communicate with Saphira and me.

"I'll take Ladon," Thorn called from below. "You take Jessie. Be careful." He took off after Ladon.

As I flew over the trees, I quickly gained on Jessie.

She was running hard and fast, better than I had before I'd shifted, but I easily kept up with her.

She jumped over the large trunk of a fallen tree and crouched in a thick section of brush.

She was up to something, and she wanted me to fly right to her.

I might not have military training, but that didn't mean I lacked critical thinking. I slowed my flight and darted a few trees over behind her.

As I moved, the sound of approaching dragon wings filled my ears, and Saphira's butterscotch dragon soared into view. She was gliding toward Thorn, and my shoulders lightened. Thorn would have backup as he chased Ladon in human form.

A *click* refocused me on Jessie. Even though Thorn was getting help, we weren't home free. I flapped my wings harder, wanting her to think I was planning to fly higher or away.

Hearing the *snick* of the trigger, I stopped moving my wings and crashed.

My body slammed into the ground, and pain exploded in my legs. I could only pray my plan had worked and she hadn't expected me to plummet. Pushing the discomfort aside, I flapped my wings hard and raced toward her. I didn't want to give her a chance to reload the gun.

That uncomfortable rumbling started in my stomach, and I knew it was fire. Boy, did it feel like indigestion. I blew flames into the brush where she was hiding. The green leaves shriveled and died from the heat.

Jessie raced out of her hiding spot, and I snaked after her, staying low to the ground while extending my talons.

When I hovered over her, she lifted her rifle and aimed at my belly.

She'd been waiting for this moment. That was why none of the warriors had shifted. They were planning to take us down with their tranqs, and I'd fallen into her trap.

As she pulled the trigger, I darted to the right behind a large red spruce. The dart barely missed my tail, but as the old saying went, *almost* didn't count. I hadn't been hit.

I twisted around, knowing she would either be out of darts or needing to reload. I had to get her to run so I could knock her out.

Then I heard Thorn scream, "Saphira, no!"

My throat went dry, and not from breathing flames.

CHAPTER TWENTY-TWO

EVERYTHING inside me screamed to rush toward them, but my dragon didn't budge. We hovered in the air, doing nothing. Clarity descended upon me as if the dragon and I were finally merging from battle. If we flew off, Jessie could call in reinforcements and have time to strategize. Right now, both sides were on even ground, making decisions in the moment. If I reacted, the odds could switch in their favor. I had to trust Thorn and Saphira to handle themselves.

Though it went against my nature, I focused on my target, channeling my frustration into catching her.

She'd gone back into her hiding spot in the thick bushes. I had to destroy it.

I pumped my wings faster, letting my dragon take control. She was better at this than I was, and I needed to stop fighting her.

The breeze cascaded over me, invigorating me as I flew toward the bush and extended my talons. A good way to fight an enemy was to prevent them from hiding.

As I drew closer, I listened for a *click* to indicate she

was readying to shoot and made my move. My talons slashed through the bushes like a knife through butter, with barely any resistance, revealing Jessie.

She was crouched with her rifle strapped to her shoulder. Instead of aiming the rifle, she held a dark metal dagger. She swung the blade at me, and my dragon form veered back, but not quickly enough: the tip of the dagger sliced the edge of my leg.

Something cold crashed through my body, numbing my magic. I dropped and landed on my butt. The ground shook...or maybe that was just my mind. My body shrank as my dragon removed herself from the center of my mind, as if she'd lost control.

Snickering, Jessie stood and tossed the rifle back into the brush to keep it hidden should someone stumble upon us. With the dagger in one hand, she removed an oversized metal bracelet from the back of her belt. "You have no idea what you're up against."

As my scales turned into skin, I felt something large heading our way, but as soon as I was human, I could no longer sense it. My magic was on the fritz.

The breeze, which had been comforting a few minutes ago, blew my hair around my shoulders, reminding me that I was sitting here buck naked. I folded my arms over my breasts and crossed my ankles, completely exposed. "How did you do that?"

She frowned. "He should've never changed you. You're clueless about this world, but that's what you get for being a greedy human." She lifted her dagger. "It's made of Wolfram Dwiin, tungsten metal forged—"

"By dragon's fire." My blood boiled at her condescending tone. "Not just *any* dragon but a royal."

Head tilting back, she scanned me again. I wished

she'd look away because I severely underdressed.

"Color me surprised, but that doesn't change what has to happen." She lifted the gigantic handcuff. "We can do this the easy way, or I'll be forced to hurt you again." She came toward me.

My skin jolted like it did any time I was close to Thorn. My dragon roared and pressed against my mind, wanting to take back control, but it was like she couldn't enter.

The sound of wings flapping made me dizzy. Considering the way my body was reacting, I was pretty sure it was Thorn. I was *attuned* to him.

Jessie snarled and turned her head toward our new arrival. Now that she was distracted, I took the opportunity to do the same.

Thorn's gorgeous dragon form soared toward us between a red spruce and Fraser fir. His plum scales glittered more silvery in the moonlight. Smoke trickled from his nose, and his sky blue eyes focused on me. He roared so loudly that my body vibrated. Then his attention locked on Jessie. He zoomed across the clearing, and I yelled, "She's got a Wolfram Dwinn dagger and a handcuff!" With his background, he probably already knew that, but I didn't want to assume and have him stuck in the same situation I was in.

Unthreatened by me, Jessie turned to Thorn. She clutched the dagger in her hand, and when Thorn got close, she swiped at him as she had with me. Unlike *me*, however, he was prepared for it. He drew his dragon legs close to his stomach...and breathed fire.

She rolled to the side, avoiding the flames, and climbed back onto her feet. She stood with her legs shoulder-width apart, waiting for Thorn to attack again.

This was why I needed to get in shape. Even at twenty-two, I was convinced that if I tried that, I'd break a hip.

My dragon grumbled, unhappy with me sitting here, covering my privates, while Thorn was under attack. She was right. I needed to do *something*.

But what?

I scanned the area and noticed that Jessie was inching back toward her hiding space. A lightbulb went off: she was moving toward her rifle so she could tranq Thorn.

Not if I got the rifle first.

Whimpering, I climbed to my feet, keeping my hands over my breasts. There wasn't much I could do about my lower half. Though I had a plan, that didn't mean I was willing to run through the woods naked. I needed to find some clothes, *pronto*, but after I took the rifle from her.

Thorn glanced at me, his eyes reflecting worry. He obviously thought something was wrong with me, which I could use to hide my intention. A strange growl emanated from his chest, sounding more threatening than his roar. I'd never heard the sound before. I still knew very little, as Jessie had reminded me.

I stumbled a few steps, trying to appear disoriented, which unfortunately wasn't hard. I suspected that it was less acting than I'd have liked to imagine.

As Thorn swooped down to attack Jessie, I walked in a zigzag, hoping like hell she didn't realize what I was doing. I was praying her entire focus was on her battle with Thorn.

The closer I got to her hiding place, the more difficult it was to hide my destination. Out of the corner of my eye, I watched as she swiped the dagger at the tip of Thorn's wing as it descended, changing her strategy. He jumped back into a tree. Her gaze landed on me.

"Oh, *hell*, no," she spat and ran toward me.

Losing all sense of modesty, I pumped my arms at my sides, rushing the last ten feet to the rifle.

The sound of wings flapping told me that Thorn was already getting into position to hold her off. With her speed, I needed every ounce of help I could get. I was *not* a fast runner, especially not in bare feet.

As I lunged for the rifle, Jessie screamed, but it could have been a distraction. I reached the thicket, unsure where she'd put the gun.

Her footsteps started toward me.

Moonlight glinted off a dark piece of metal, and I snatched up the rifle. As I straightened, a body slammed into me, knocking me into a tree trunk behind the bushes. I kept my grip firm on the rifle, not willing to lose it, and as I steadied myself, Jessie punched me in the cheek. My head snapped sideways, the pain blinding. I'd never been in a fight before, except for the one with the cliff before Thorn changed me.

My dragon surged, brushing my mind, and instinctively, I jabbed the butt of the rifle into Jessie's side. She stumbled back a few steps. Thorn appeared above her, and his talons dug into her shoulders and lifted her off the ground.

She smirked sickeningly as she raised her dagger.

I lifted the rifle, aimed at her chest, and pulled the trigger, hoping the gun was loaded.

I chanted internally, *Please don't hit Thorn.*

A tranq shot out of the barrel, and I held my breath. Jessie stabbed him in the leg a moment before the dart hit her calf.

Not exactly the spot I'd been going for, but at least it had hit *somewhere.*

Thorn's huge form shrank as the metal took effect, and he tumbled from the sky. He released Jessie, and she crashed like dead weight. Thorn still had wings and lowered himself to the ground before dropping the remaining ten feet.

Saliva filled my mouth as I hurried over to him. There was no telling how deep she'd cut him. I dropped to my knees at his side and pushed the hair from his eyes. I murmured, "Thorn?" I didn't want to be too loud in case someone else was close by.

Our skin sizzled, and his eyelids cracked open, revealing his beautiful, glowing eyes. My own burned with unshed tears. Thank goodness he was at least coherent.

"Jessie!" he exclaimed, sitting upright quickly.

I became very aware that he was *naked.* And so was I. My eyes acted on their own will and scanned his large body. And boy, did I mean *large.* Most might even say gigantic, and not in just one thing. *Everything* about him was large. His chiseled abs, the curves of his muscles, and his pleasure seeker.

I cringed. What was I, an old lady or a young teenager? I was studying to be a *doctor*, for goodness' sake. I should be able to call it by its *technical* name—penis.

He stood, putting his pleasure seek—er, penis right in front of my face. If anyone saw us, they'd find me on my knees in front of him and get a *very* wrong idea about what was going on. Unless they saw the unconscious body several feet from us...and that would either make them realize something weird was going on or make them think we were super kinky.

Why couldn't I get my mind out of the gutter?

"I...uh..." I couldn't concentrate, so I jumped to my feet. Clearly, that had been a bad idea. Now his gaze was on my breasts.

Something spicy filled the air, making me salivate.

Jessie groaned, slamming me back into the present. I needed clothes for him and me as soon as possible.

"I tranqed her." I lifted the rifle, refocusing his attention before we got too distracted, or worse, I mumbled something about his pleasure seeker. Then I remembered him hollering Saphira's name. "Where's Saphira? Is she okay?"

"She'll be here soon." He cleared his throat and jerked his head away. "I'm sorry if we worried you, but I had to distract Ladon, so I yelled. She stayed to fight him while I shifted and came to check on you."

I licked my lips. "How are we supposed to get out of this situation?" I waved my hand at him and me. "How long until we can shift back into dragons?"

"Just a few minutes." He ran a hand through his hair, his bicep bulging. "You might be able to shift now. The fumes prick the skin and vanish rather quickly. They do that to force a shift and then put on a Wolfram Dwinn collar."

My world dizzied. If a room covered in Wolfram Dwinn could stop someone from shifting, I'd bet a collar would do the same.

Wings whirred toward us, and Thorn and I turned in the direction he had come from. I spotted a hint of butterscotch scales.

Saphira.

Some of the weight on my shoulders disappeared. She was all right and heading toward us. "I'm so glad to see her." I ignored my dragon and the part of me that was not thrilled about her seeing Thorn naked. This was a high-stakes situation, so our safety was more important than me worrying about her seeing him.

"Ladon was injured. I know you care about her, and I wouldn't have left her unless I was sure she could handle things," Thorn assured me with a sad smile, and my heart skipped a beat.

He was so damn handsome that even a painting couldn't capture his perfection. But I feared that if I didn't try once things were settled, I'd never be able to remember him well enough. It was inevitable that we'd part, even if I didn't want that. I'd learned the hard way that wishes and desires didn't change a damn thing. In certain cases, like with Thorn, they only broke your heart, time and time again.

"I know," I said softly, not questioning if he could hear me.

Adoration filled his eyes, but then it vanished. "Why don't you try to shift again? We need to get out of here." He turned his back to me, and my heart panged.

Now wasn't the time to push him. We could be attacked again at any moment. Anything I wanted to say to him could wait. But what was the point? We wouldn't be with each other much longer.

Pushing away my trivial concerns and focusing on our safety, I inhaled deeply and let my dragon brush my mind once more. This time, she was able to enter it, and her magic thrummed through me. My body grew larger as I stumbled away from Thorn and shifted.

If Thorn couldn't shift soon, I would carry him back to the cabin.

As Saphira approached, she snarled and darted the last ten yards toward us.

I noticed something to my left, behind the trunk of a red spruce: a rifle lifting in our direction.

Falkor.

My human side froze, but thank goodness for my dragon. She sprang to life.

I roared and took flight, using one of my legs to shove Thorn out of the way. He hit the ground hard.

As I leaped toward Falkor, he turned the gun on me. He pulled the trigger, but Saphira appeared, blocking me from the tranq. The thud of the dart lodging into her scales rang in my ears. Instead of crashing, she flew toward Falkor. She roared, and my dragon understood what she was telling me.

She wanted us to go.

Her wings slowed, and her body shrank. There was no way I could reach her to carry her out of here. Not with Falkor right there.

"Everly, go. I still can't shift," Thorn said behind me. "You need to get out of here."

If he thought I was leaving without him, he would soon learn otherwise. Turning, I swooped down and picked up Thorn in my front claws. I flapped my wings hard, pushing myself to get us out of this hellhole.

When Saphira's body fell to the ground, my heart stopped. She'd sacrificed herself to give us a chance to get away.

We broke through the treetops, my heart squeezing as if it were trapped in a vise. I hated that I'd left Saphira behind.

"Don't slow down," Thorn commanded. "We aren't alone."

CHAPTER TWENTY-THREE

HIS WORDS ECHOED in my head, but I couldn't sense anyone chasing after us. Falkor had Saphira down below.

Then my dragon senses alerted me that Falkor's form was getting bigger.

A lump formed in my throat. Falkor was the person in command. I wasn't sure how *I* was supposed to go up against him.

Pumping my wings as fast as they'd go, I soared back toward the cabin, Thorn fidgeting in my grip. Even though I couldn't see him and I was four times his size, I could feel the hard cut of his muscles where my toes wrapped around him, and the lightning jolt between us was sparking throughout my body.

I was unsure what to do, and I wished I could talk to him. However, remembering how slowly I'd run, I didn't want to land and shift back into human form. In this state, I could move faster than on my human legs.

"Listen to me," Thorn said as he placed his hands on my top claw. "You have a head start and can fly fast.

Push yourself, and don't head straight back to the cabin, or we'll lead them right to us. They can follow our scent."

Oh, great. So I was going to be flying around forever while holding his naked body. I cringed. That didn't sound horrible, except for the warrior chasing us.

My goodness. My hormones were getting the best of me, and we were in a life-or-death situation. I'd heard lust made you stupid, and I could attest to that fact, unfortunately.

I made a strange noise, a cross between a groan and a growl. Instinct told me to go in the opposite direction, but that would lead us closer to the dragons that supported the king and Drake, which wasn't smart.

What was a girl to do?

My dragon took control just as Falkor crested the trees. She turned my body toward Asheville. I almost fought her, but then awareness seeped into me.

If we were around humans, Falkor would behave better. And, dare I say, he might have to give up the chase. The only problem was that Thorn and I would be *naked* in the middle of the city.

That was better than death.

Unless a woman saw Thorn naked. Saphira and Jessie were bad enough. My tolerance of more women seeing him this way had vanished.

That split personality I felt whenever I thought of Thorn fought against itself. I'd hoped that things would get better, but this sire bond situation was strengthening instead of subsiding. I wasn't sure what to do about it since staying away from him wasn't an option right now.

I flew higher, ensuring no one could see us. There was a reason dragons hadn't exposed themselves to humans yet, though I wasn't certain what it was. Another question I'd eventually want answered.

Falkor roared as his wings flapped urgently, showing his desperation to catch us. Every part of him was green except for the undersides of his wings, which were burnt orange. He looked like a warrior dragon, moving gracefully and precisely, his entire focus on me.

"Stop watching him," Thorn commanded, his body tense. "It'll slow you down. Trust your dragon—she's part of you now—and move."

Looking forward again as we headed toward Asheville, I obeyed Thorn and repeated to myself what he'd said. At first, my dragon and I had felt like separate beings, but the gap was narrowing. We were at odds about little things, especially when it came to *him*. He was the driving force that made my two sides fight each other, which had to be from the sire bond or whatever the dragon version of that was called.

I shoved that portion of my dragon and my bond from my mind, wanting us to work in tandem.

Falkor's bulky frame was slowly catching up to us. My lungs struggled to fill as my dragon pushed us harder. We picked up a little speed, but all that accomplished was keeping Falkor the same distance away. I wasn't putting more distance between us.

The starry night was still gorgeous. The colors I'd marveled at before swirled around us, and the air smelled clean, like before a good snow. The temperature was colder up here, high in the sky where no human could see us shrouded in darkness.

One day, I wanted to fly when we weren't in danger. It was freeing, especially with the surrounding sky lights so beautiful to be part of.

"Where are we heading?" Thorn asked below me.

I wanted to roll my eyes but didn't waste the energy, especially since he couldn't see the gesture. Instead, I nodded toward the lights of the place where I'd spent my whole life. Though we were still twenty miles away, we could see the gorgeous mountain city. Although it was one in the morning, the lights were bright, illuminating its beauty.

He cleared his throat. "Everly, I don't know what you're planning, but we can't let humans know about us. Even though we're stronger, there are more humans than dragons, and they have military weapons at their disposal. They'd likely try to eliminate or control us."

His assumption that I was planning to expose us boded well. It was exactly what I wanted Falkor to suspect.

I began my descent. This late, there weren't any cars driving below, but I wanted to get close enough so that if Falkor did damn near catch us, we could use the small population of people who were out this late to distract him. The threat of me outing us to the human world had to count for something with him. I suspected the king wouldn't be happy about it, or the world would already know about dragons.

Behind us, Falkor growled, maybe to communicate his concern.

A memory floated through my mind, giving me an idea. I darted downward, not wanting to risk getting any closer. We were ten miles shy of the outskirts of the city. I barreled toward an area where Mom had often forced me to hike with her. It had yielded the prettiest pictures, which we'd used as inspiration for our paintings. A sizable spring surfaced nearby. Its stream went on for miles and ran into a large waterfall that was popular with tourists during the day, but at night, that shouldn't be an issue. Not that I planned to go *that* far.

With the lead we had on Falkor, I should be able to drop into the spring and shift into human form. Hopefully, we could use the water to hide us and mask our scent.

My dragon pushed harder, and the trickle of water over the rocks caught my ear. Luckily, it was May, which meant there was more rain than normal and the water level was higher. Exactly what we needed.

As I breezed through two stands of red spruce, my dragon withdrew from my mind, and something pinged my dragon senses, but the shift back into human was already underway. All I could tell before I lost my awareness was that it was a couple of large animals, likely bears. At least Falkor couldn't see us now that we were just above the water.

"Let me go," Thorn rasped. He knew I was struggling to keep him in my grip.

Even though I didn't want to drop him, I didn't have a choice. As my body shrank to half my dragon size, he slipped from my reforming hands. My wings kept me from completely descending so I wouldn't land on top of him.

As he crashed into the water, my body completed the transformation, and I dropped the remaining five feet after him. I gulped a breath moments before I splashed into the frigid waters. Thank goodness I was a dragon, or I'd be freezing.

At first, I was disoriented. I'd never been a strong swimmer, but I was good enough not to drown. I hoped there might be campers around, or hunters, to prevent Falkor from combing the area too long.

My vision was clear, but the water was murky with mud from the recent rains. I could feel ripples coming from Thorn swimming a few feet in front of me. I waited for my lungs to burn from holding my breath too long, but instead, a strong arm grabbed my waist, and before I realized what was going on, Thorn had pressed me against his body. The world spun from the lightning jolt between us, but he guided me to a spot and brought us up for air. Then I realized that this part of the spring was lined by thick brush instead of the rocks I was used to. Clearly, Mom and I had never seen this section of the spring.

We hunkered shoulder-deep in the water, our heads just above the surface and shielded by branches and our bodies hidden by the murky water. Even dragons couldn't see through dirt, but Falkor would sense us if we weren't careful.

I tried to stay still and held my breath as Falkor swooped into view. My mouth went dry as a scream bottled in my throat. I needed to swallow, but I remained frozen, afraid to move a muscle.

"You all, stay in the tent," a man said, sounding concerned. I estimated he was about a quarter mile away. "I'll check things out to make sure we're safe here. If I scream to run, you take the kids to the car, Joy."

My heart hammered. Those "bears" were actually human campers. My dragon had tried to alert me before she'd retreated, and I hadn't picked up on what they were. However, Falkor could.

Falkor relented with a low growl of disgust, but he soon ascended into the sky to get away before the human reached us. I wanted to run away, too, but we needed to stay here a little longer to make sure Falkor was too far away to spot us.

"We're not out of the woods yet," Thorn murmured.

I flicked my attention to his face, the worst thing I could have done. I was pressed against his chest, naked, and now my eyes were focused on his mouth. I licked my lips, desperate to taste his, and need slammed into my body. Even the frigid waters of the spring couldn't smother the fire raging inside me.

He hissed, his irises glowing. Then I wrapped my legs around his waist.

Yeah, I'd lost my mind. I was climbing my kidnapper, who'd changed me into a dragon, while we were hiding from another dragon, naked, in the water with a human checking out the area. Those were things I'd *never* imagined would apply to me.

"Dammit, Ev," Thorn growled as his lips captured mine.

The world faded away, and I could only vaguely hear the human coming closer through the darkness as Thorn and I devoured each other. His tongue swept over mine, and I clung to him. He tasted minty, even after breathing fire, and each stroke and touch made the world fade further from my mind.

He gripped my hips and pressed his pleasure seeker against me.

"Who's there?" the man asked from the embankment, and reality filtered back into my mind.

My face burned. We should've been quiet, but we'd gotten caught up in kissing and crushing our bodies together.

Thorn laid his forehead against mine and closed his eyes.

The man swept a flashlight right where we were hiding and said, "Come out, or I'm calling the cops."

For him to know exactly where we were indicated we'd been making more noise than I'd realized.

"Stay here," Thorn murmured as he untangled me from his body.

I came close to whimpering. I didn't want to release him, but we definitely didn't need to get the cops involved. I behaved and placed both feet on the rocky spring bed, sinking into the water.

"Hey, sorry." Thorn stepped out of our hiding spot into view of the flashlight. "I...decided to go for a late-night skinny dip and don't want you to see my dangly bits."

My shoulders shook with quiet laughter. He hadn't lied, making his delivery sincere.

The man's stern face relaxed, and his brows furrowed. "The water is still cold this time of year. You need to get out before you get sick."

"I will." Thorn pushed his wet bangs out of his eyes. "I heard something else out here, but I think whatever it was is gone."

The man rolled his shoulders. "Yeah, it must have been an animal." He turned to head back to his family but paused. "Do you need help? I have a cell phone if you need to call someone."

Times like these restored some of my faith in people. Most people I'd come into contact with had wanted me for *something*. To help them make a good grade, cover a shift at the coffee shop, or go away. This man...this *human*...was concerned about Thorn, even though he didn't know him.

"Nah, my girl is around here somewhere. I need to get back to her, but thank you," Thorn said kindly.

"Yeah, okay. But seriously, get out of the water." The man turned away and hurried back to his family.

When he was out of sight, Thorn rushed to me. "We need to shift and fly around before heading back to the cabin. He may still call the cops."

"Okay." If I were that man, I'd call the cops and have them come by to make sure Thorn was okay and not doing anything shady. The man was far enough away that if we shifted and flew off quickly, he probably wouldn't notice us.

Without another word, we let our dragons take control. After the man got back into his tent, we took flight, careful to watch for Falkor.

Luckily, there was no sign of him, but the tightness in my stomach wouldn't release. Even though Thorn and I had gotten away unscathed, Saphira had likely been captured, and Thorn's parents were still locked up. We'd already burned a day, and we had less than twenty-four hours to determine another plan before Thorn had to choose to turn himself in or risk his parents' lives.

I already knew which one he would choose: he'd give himself up.

My heart fractured. The world *needed* him. He was the light that a corrupt king wanted to extinguish.

Even flying didn't feel as nice with the weight of the situation on my mind. We'd hoped to get answers, to determine a solution, but all we'd done was tip them off that we were trying to save his parents without Thorn turning himself in.

After a few hours of flying around in every direction

to confuse any dragon that might be tracking us, we arrived back in the woods in front of the cabin.

The two of us shifted into human form, not bothering to hide from each other.

As we entered the warm cabin, I hugged myself. The urge to ogle Thorn surged through me, but I kept my eyes averted to the floor. I was about to ask him where the clothes were when Thorn cleared his throat.

I glanced up into his eyes...and the world went still. A sweet, spicy scent swirled between us, and the lightning bolt shot down my center, even though we weren't touching.

At the same time, we closed the distance between us. I stood on my tiptoes to reach his lips, but he whispered, "Wait. We need to talk."

CHAPTER TWENTY-FOUR

I STOPPED BREATHING. A shiver ran down my spine like a cold shower. His words were more frigid than the spring waters we'd been in hours ago and didn't bode well for a happy conversation, especially not when the two people involved were naked.

Though everything inside me wanted to rub my body all over Thorn, I forced myself to step back. I crossed my arms over my breasts and turned half away so I could conceal most of my full-frontal view. However, my traitorous eyes kept trying to scan his body, and I became disgusted with myself. I understood how a guy might struggle when a woman said, "My eyes are up here."

But if I went to get dressed, Thorn might change his mind about saying whatever he wanted to say. If he was going to reject the idea of us, I needed to hear him say it. Otherwise, I would continue to pine for a man who wasn't interested in me. It was better to have my heart shattered than continue to hope.

Hope made you do foolish things.

"Sure." I straightened my shoulders, trying not to look awkward and self-conscious.

He grimaced and scratched the back of his head.

My heartbeat quickened, but not from desire like before. Sweat pooled around my hairline, and I wanted him to spit it out so we could get dressed. Well, okay, I didn't really want *him* to get dressed, but that was the problem. "Here. I'll help you out. You aren't interested in me." As soon as I'd said the words, I wanted to take them back. "Not that we have a future, anyway." My dragon roared in anger so loudly that I nearly clutched my head.

His face twisted in agony, and he exhaled.

I was making things worse. But this was the first time I'd felt like this toward anyone, and the feelings were strong and all-encompassing and making me stupid. So what did I do? I continued to talk. "Because I have to go back to Drake and be—"

A low growl rumbled from his chest as he stalked toward me and wrapped his arms around my waist, pulling me flush against him again. He rasped, "Do *not* finish that sentence."

My body warmed again from the lightning shooting between us. My brain fuzzed as I tried to remember that he'd put the brakes on things. I shook my head, needing to do something other than *kiss* him. He'd essentially said no, and I would never force myself on anyone.

"I'm just saying you don't have to explain. I understand that you don't want to complicate matters." I licked my lips, tasting him. I tried to sear it into my mind, along with his features. I suspected I'd be reliving these stolen moments for the rest of my life, and I needed to remember as many as possible. The mind had a way of darkening memories.

He smirked, but the humor didn't reach his eyes. "You think things can get any more complicated? My thoughts revolve around you. You've already become the center of my world."

I gulped as tingles and the thrumming of our connection erupted all over my body. I grew light-headed from the high, and I never wanted to come down. But I had to remain logical. He'd pulled away for a reason. "Then why did you stop me from kissing you?"

"I need to make sure you understand the consequences," he murmured as he cupped my face. "That we have a special connection, and it will only strengthen, especially if we make love."

A shudder ran through me. The fact that he'd called it *making love* instead of *having sex* made my stomach flip-flop. He was also trying to tell me about our sire bond. "I already know."

His brows rose. "What? How?"

I stared into his gorgeous irises and replied, "I feel our connection through my entire body. It's like you're anchored to my soul."

His breath caught. "I'm sorry. I didn't know it would happen."

"Stop apologizing." I wrapped my arms around his neck and twisted my fingers in his hair. My breasts pressed into his chest, and my body thrummed with hot desire. "You *saved* me, and you tried to change me back into a human. If it weren't for you, I'd be dead, and I'm sorry I reacted so strongly. Even if our feelings are making this situation messy, I wouldn't change a moment of our time together, including the rough start."

Adoration filled his face as he stared into my soul. He

whispered, "Same. I wish our meeting had been different."

My heart ached. "Me, too, but right now, I need you to shut up and kiss me."

His hands cupped my ass as his breathing turned ragged. "Ev, are you sure—"

The nickname expelled the last of my sanity, and I pressed my lips to his. "Yes. Now take care of me."

"Always," he promised and returned my kiss with vigor.

That wasn't a promise he could make, but I pushed the negative thought away. He and I deserved a night together. Even if, tomorrow, it would change everything.

I parted my lips, and his tongue entered my mouth. His faint vanilla taste filled my senses. He lifted me by my ass and, with one hand, made sure the front door was locked before hurrying down the hallway into the first bedroom. The one I hadn't been in before—his.

He laid me down on the mattress gently and quickly climbed up beside me without breaking our kiss once. A hand inched down my stomach, and he pulled away from my mouth to suck on one of my nipples.

My body quivered, and I trailed my fingers along his abs, enjoying his attention and the hard curves of his body. He was more perfect than any sculpture, and I was thrilled that I was one of the few who would be able to enjoy it. My dragon growled at the thought of him with anyone else, and some of the pleasure dimmed.

He went still and straightened. "Did I do something wrong?"

"What?" I couldn't process the question because it was so absurd. "God, no. What you're doing is perfect. It's just...I couldn't help but think about why you know exactly what to do."

Jaw going slack, he blinked twice. "You think I've done this before?"

My body tensed. "Well, look at you. I mean—"

"Ev, I've been hiding my entire life and keeping everyone but my parents at arm's length." He smiled tenderly. "If I'm doing anything right, it's solely because of our connection."

His confession had my body melting, and I refused to think about our future. At least this was something we could share with each other. "I'm a virgin, too."

He beamed, and I forgot how to breathe. He was that damn perfect. My body ached for him in a way that was almost too painful.

"No more talking," I whispered as I kissed him.

He chuckled deeply, and my body blazed. In this moment, he seemed truly happy, and I was going to allow myself to believe it was because of me.

His fingers slipped between my legs, and he circled a sensitive spot that forced me to stop kissing him and lean my head back. Wanting to give him the same type of pleasure, I touched his shaft, thrilled with what I found. He was just as ready for me.

Mouth on my breasts, he worked my body like an artist creating a masterpiece. The friction slowly built as his scent and taste filled my entire world.

He moaned as he circled my spot faster, and my body exploded with pleasure...but it wasn't enough. I pulled away from him, and he hissed in disappointment.

"I'm not done with you—" he protested until I straddled him and lowered myself so he entered me. He grabbed my waist and murmured, "Slow down. Don't hurt yourself."

My chest expanded. Instead of worrying about his own pleasure, he wanted to take care of me. "Don't worry, I won't. But it's my turn to pleasure you."

His pupils slitted, and my stomach clenched with unfathomable need.

Even if I hadn't wanted to take my time, I didn't have much choice. He was gigantic, and I had to continually let myself adjust to him for a few seconds before lowering myself another inch. He scooted to the headboard and sat up as the dark purple sheets bunched around us.

"You're so damn beautiful," he said as he lowered his head to my breasts.

As his tongue stroked my nipples, warmth curled in my stomach, and I finally got him all the way inside me. I moved my hips, the burn of my first time a little uncomfortable, but after a few thrusts, that discomfort was replaced with something mind-blowing. I increased our pace.

Thorn leaned back against the headboard and clutched my waist. "Oh, gods. You feel so damn amazing," he groaned as he bucked underneath me.

Our bodies slick with sweat, we moved in rhythm. If I hadn't known better, I'd have believed we'd had sex many times. He knew exactly what I wanted, and each one of his sighs and moans encouraged me.

Friction built inside me, and my body clenched as if preparing for an explosion. I locked eyes with him, his irises glowing as his pupils elongated and his dragon peeked through.

My dragon stirred in response.

"I love you," he confessed, his sincerity in every line of his face.

Despite the short amount of time we'd spent together, there was no question about how I felt in return. "I love you, too."

Another orgasm ripped through my body, and he pumped harder, his body shaking from his release.

Something inside me *snapped*. Suddenly, his emotions and mine intermingled. The ecstasy intensified, his pleasure mixing with mine, and the world shook. Our dragons roared in unison, the way our two halves were meant to be.

I wasn't sure if it was minutes or hours, but it didn't matter—the amount of time wasn't long enough as our bodies quieted and stopped thrumming with bliss. I sank onto his chest, and he wrapped his arms around me.

At least we had this moment, I thought.

His arms tensed. *We'll have these moments repeatedly for the rest of our lives.*

I stiffened and tried to roll off him, but he held me tightly. I'd heard his dragon in my head just moments ago, but I'd been so drunk on our sex high that I hadn't paid attention. Now I was hearing his voice in my head, too. "Why can I hear you?"

He turned us to one side so we were facing each other and smiled tenderly. "Because of our connection. We've completed the bond."

None of that made sense. My heart dropped. "You're going to have sex with every human you turn into a dragon?"

He blinked, and his brows furrowed. "What? No! You're my *first*, *last*, and *only*. Why would you think that?

Not that I'm planning to turn any more humans into dragons, anyway."

"Because of the sire bond." Some of my hurt ebbed, but not my confusion. "I thought it was formed from you changing someone, but I guess you have to have sex with them, too."

"Sire bond?" His nose wrinkled. "What in the *hell* are you talking about? We don't have a *sire* bond."

I felt incredibly stupid. "But...after you changed me, my attraction to you increased a hundredfold. Since then, it's been getting stronger."

"You thought it was because I changed you?" His arms loosened. "Gods, no. At first, I was surprised by how I responded to you when you were human, but once you became a dragon, everything clicked into place." His hand rested on my cheek, the lightning bolt surging between us.

I would never get tired of this. "Mind filling me in?"

"When you were human, we were soulmates," he whispered.

Soulmates. The very thing so many stories and movies were made about. A person designed specifically for you. "Were? What are we now?"

"Fated mates," he said softly, his irises lightening to the shade of blue that was quickly becoming my favorite. "Two halves of the same soul. Now that you're a dragon, too, we've completed the bond, and our souls are merged. We are linked for the rest of our lives."

I loved the sound of that...except we wouldn't have that opportunity. "What happens when I have to hand myself over to Drake? Will he know?"

Thorn's nostrils flared as he held me tight. He damn near bellowed, "You will *not* be handing yourself over to Drake. You are *mine*, and I won't share you with anyone."

All my life, I'd known that I would never put up with someone being possessive. Oh, yet again, how wrong I was. My throat actually emitted a purring sound.

That noise must have calmed Thorn because he smiled at me and chuckled. "Did you like that, babe?"

Babe.

Between all the sensations coursing through my chest and my stomach, I was beginning to worry I had indigestion. That would be very unfortunate. "Kinda, but I never thought I would."

"Humans think it's unhealthy because the jackasses who are like that are usually controlling. But not with shifters. We're possessive because we love the other person so much, it makes us crazy thinking about someone else touching them, harming them, upsetting them." He kissed my nose. "I want you to be happy, and if that takes cutting off Drake's testicles to ensure he has no use for you, I'm more than happy to do it."

I giggled, the sound foreign and unfamiliar. For this brief moment, I was high on all things Thorn.

"And that right there is what I plan to do every day for the rest of our lives." He tucked a piece of my blonde hair behind my ear. "Make you smile and laugh."

Tears threatened to spill as my throat thickened. I was blissfully happy, but doom was around the corner, choking me. "We both know that can't happen."

Jaw clenching, Thorn rolled on top of me, pinning me underneath him. He rasped, "You will *not* be getting close to Drake. We will figure out another solution. Giving you up is *not* an option."

There was so much power in his voice that I believed him. Thorn was a kind and loyal man but viciously protective of those he loved. And now I was one of them.

Maybe we *could* find a way to keep my sister safe and save his parents and Saphira. I nodded, staring at his full lips.

"Good," he murmured and kissed me.

My body was already warming for round two. I wrapped my legs around him, eager for him to slide in.

He groaned and pulled back. *No, you need a chance to heal first. This was your first time, and even though I want to claim you again, I need to take care of you better.* He pouted as he reached behind his back and untangled my legs from his body. *Go take a shower. I'll change the sheets and make us something to eat before we sleep. We need to rest so we can figure out what to do next.*

All the lightheartedness vanished. The threat hung over us again, and even though I wanted to sex him up, I *was* sore. A warm shower would do me good. "Fine, but we will do this again soon."

"Definitely." He winked.

He stood and took my hands, helping me to my feet. His voice said in my head, *Now go take a shower before you make me* not *treat you like the special treasure you are.*

My heart skipped a beat. The way I felt about him shouldn't have been possible, but I loved him more than anything else in this world. *Fine.* I glanced at the bed, wanting to see visual evidence of our time together, and noted blood on his sheets.

I cringed. No wonder he wanted to get out of bed and change the linens. *I'm sorry.*

He placed his finger under my chin, forcing me to look him in the eyes. "That is the most wonderful thing that could've happened." He motioned to the bloodstain. "Don't you *dare* apologize for it."

Warmth poured through my chest, near my heart, as

his love and sincerity filled me. My cheeks hurt from grinning ear to ear. He'd said I was his special treasure, and I felt like just that.

He grabbed my shoulders and turned me toward his bathroom, then smacked my ass. "Get into the shower, and when you come out, head to the kitchen. I'll make us some grilled cheese sandwiches and vegetable soup."

As he left the room, my stomach gurgled in anticipation.

Now that I wasn't staring at him, I took in the space. It didn't tell me more about him. The room had the exact same layout as mine, with the same wall color and furniture style, though his bed had purple sheets.

I quickly entered the bathroom, not wanting to be apart from him for long. His was double the size of mine and Saphira's. There was a much bigger sink with a cabinet underneath it, and a tub about three times larger.

In other words, we could have shower sex.

Wow. I had a one-track mind.

I opened the cabinet and found several clean towels. I snatched one and threw it over the shower rod. The shower curtain's shimmery light blue color reminded me of Thorn's eyes.

Eager to get back to him, I hurried through my shower, taking enough time to clean myself without dawdling.

When I entered the bedroom, I paused. I found the duffel bag I'd packed to take at Drake's at the foot of the bed. I connected, *My stuff.*

I figured I was long overdue giving it back to you, he replied, a twinge of regret floating through. *And I thought you might like to check in with your siblings.*

I love you, I connected and hurried to my bag. *You*

were doing what you had to do for those you love. I snatched my favorite pair of pajamas from the bag—a shirt and shorts that resembled a colorful abstract oil painting with various shades of blue, yellow, and orange. Once I was dressed, I dug out my phone and charger. As expected, the battery was dead.

The warmth in my chest chilled, and I understood what that meant. Something had upset Thorn.

I hurried toward him. When I stepped into the living room, my eyes locked on him. He was sitting in front of a laptop but frowning at his phone, his back rigid.

When the screen from his cell phone came into view, my knees nearly gave out. I muttered, "Oh, no."

CHAPTER TWENTY-FIVE

AS I DROPPED, Thorn spun around and wrapped an arm around my waist, pulling me against him. The jolt of our connection thrummed between us, but all I could do was gape at the phone's screen.

Saphira.

She wore the collar I'd mistaken for a handcuff around her neck. The dark Wolfram Dwiin metal shone against her skin. She had cuts on her face and a black eye. They'd beaten her after forcing her to shift back into her human form.

She stood in the middle of a grove of red spruces and Fraser firs, which didn't help pinpoint where she was. The trees were common throughout the Blue Ridge Mountains, and the woods were everywhere.

"Thorn, who sent that?" I rasped, my lungs barely moving. I wanted to shut down, but that wouldn't get either one of them out of this situation.

His hand tightened around my waist, and he answered, "It was texted to me a minute ago. I thought it was from King Arman about my parents, but I was wrong."

My throat hurt, but I forced myself to swallow. "What do you mean? Who is it?"

He turned my body toward him and rasped, "It's Drake. Somehow, he got my number."

I furrowed my brows. "But why would he think you care about Saphira? Unless—"

"The message was for both of us," he finished as his face scrunched in agony. "He's trying to get a rise out of you since his efforts haven't worked on me so far."

That might be true, but I still needed to watch it. "Replay it."

He shook his head. "That's not a good idea."

My jaw twitched as boiling anger swirled around me and leaked into the connection we'd formed. I growled, "Correct me if I'm wrong, but I didn't ask for your opinion."

He flinched, and his hurt wafted through me. He inhaled slowly and straightened his shoulders. "I know that. I want to protect you."

I tensed as my heart sank. "I'm sorry, I didn't mean to snap at you." I'd reminded myself of my stepdad, and that was definitely not how Thorn should be treated. He was a good man, and I should've known his reluctance was coming from a place of concern. "It's just...*seeing* her like that..." My gaze went back to his phone, the screen dark due to inactivity.

Warmth seeped into me, and he stepped to the side so his face blocked where I'd been looking. He said, "Believe me, I get it. That's why I'm *encouraging* you not to watch it." He took my hand and placed it against his chest where I could feel his heart beating.

The *thump-thump* was better at calming me than even painting, but it didn't change anything.

I pressed my lips together as I stared at him with such adoration. He was trying to protect me, but I was a grown woman, and I couldn't be protected from everything. "If you saw a video of someone you cared about who'd been beaten up, would you listen to me if I told you not to watch it? That it was for your own good?"

His eyes narrowed. "That's playing dirty, Ev. And not the kind of dirty I approve of."

Snorting, I couldn't help but smile. "Because you know the answer."

"I would be adamant that I needed to watch it. For clues, if nothing else." He dropped his forehead to mine and whispered, "But I would still encourage you to try a different strategy."

"Noted, but *this* certain piece of advice will be ignored." I placed a hand on his cheek and pressed a quick kiss to his lips. I connected, *But I did listen, if that counts for anything.*

It does. He pulled away, frowning deeply. *That won't make this any easier.*

My mouth dried. The video had to be bad if he was that eager for me not to watch it. But if I didn't and something happened to either one of them, I would never forgive myself.

He interlocked our fingers and led me to the table, then swiped the phone and pressed play.

On the screen, Drake strolled next to Saphira, all decked out in a black suit with a sinister smile on his cruel, hardened face. I wasn't sure how I'd ever found him attractive. This was the face of a *monster*.

He wrapped an arm around Saphira's neck, placing

his face close to hers. Saphira flinched, and he chuckled as his onyx irises glowed.

The jackass was getting off on her fear.

He stared straight into the camera, and I could've sworn his gaze locked on me.

"I learned some unfortunate news tonight." He forced a frown, but his irises couldn't hide his mirth. "Something that belongs to me may have willingly aided my mortal enemy."

Acid roiled in my stomach. He had no problem making the fact that he viewed me as his property clear to anyone who watched this.

"Because I feel that aid was coerced, I'll give you one last chance." He refocused on whoever was recording. "Despite you becoming a *dragon* shifter, I'm still willing to keep our bargain. You come here and be *mine*, and I'll let Saphira go back to her father. I hear you two have become close, so it's that simple."

He steepled his fingers. "Your deadline is the same as my enemy's. You have a little over twenty-four hours. If you and the *abomination* don't show, then Cassidy, Vlad, and Saphira will lose their lives." He smirked.

Something *cracked*, and I glanced down to find that I'd broken the top piece of wood on the chair in half. I couldn't muster up the energy to care, but I released my hold.

"*Thorn*. Everly. The meeting spot is still where this story began." Drake tugged on his suit jacket. "I'll have guards there, waiting for you whenever you decide to return." He turned to walk off camera, then paused. "As long as it's before your deadline." He winked, and the video ended.

Black smoke trickled in front of me.

Thorn's strong arm wrapped around me, pulling me to his chest. Our bond thrummed between us and eased some of the turmoil in my soul, helping me see the situation more clearly.

I'm sorry, Thorn connected as he ran a hand over the back of my head. *This is all my fault.*

He didn't get to take the blame for this. I pulled back and homed in on his eyes. "Did you force Drake to find a breeder?"

His head jerked back. "Of course not."

"Did you call the king and tell him where to find your parents?" I arched a brow.

"Again, no." He searched the room as if to understand why I was asking these questions.

For someone so smart, he was missing the point. "Oh. Wait. Did you beg to be born with your extra magical powers?"

"Gods, no." He cringed. "Until this past week, I would've given anything to be a normal dragon."

I blinked. "Until this past week?"

"Yeah." He smiled tenderly. "Until you. *All* of this was worthwhile because by changing you, I revealed my fated mate. Our bond would've worked with you in human form. We would've still maintained a connection, but not one as strong as this." He brushed his thumb over my bottom lip. "Not one where we can mind link and be as close as two souls can possibly get."

My heart expanded to the point of physically hurting. That was the most romantic thing I'd *ever* heard anyone say.

He grinned, obviously feeling how his words had affected me.

But he was derailing me from my point.

"You didn't force Drake to take a breeder, you didn't rat out your parents, and you didn't ask for your magic." I held up three fingers. "Please explain why you're apologizing and saying this is all your fault?"

His face fell, but his arms tightened around me. He linked, *You're playing dirty again. If you keep doing that, we'll need to adjust things so you're only like that in bed.*

Desire flared inside me, but I had to tamp it down. We had to save Saphira and Thorn's parents. Sex would have to wait. "I'm being rational, and if we're going to save them, you've got to start thinking that way, too."

"You're right," he said and released me. "We need to eat and sleep so we can *both* think clearly. The good thing is that all three of them are dragons, and Vlad is a warrior." He removed two plates from the counter that held grilled cheeses wrapped in aluminum foil to keep them warm. Then he ladled soup into two bowls. He placed them on the kitchen table, where two glasses of water were already positioned, and moved the broken chair out of the way. "And what did that chair ever do to you?"

I chuckled and went to the outlet under the window to plug in my phone before taking a spot in front of one of the servings of food. "Wrong time and place is all. I'll figure out how to fix it."

"I'll handle it." He sat in the spot next to me.

The two of us ate in silence.

I hated to bring up the video again, but I still didn't know so much. "Where does he mean by meeting where it all began?"

"That's easy." He took a bite, which equated to half of the grilled cheese. "The place where Vlad attacked us."

"Not where you took your da—er, King Arman's dragon?" To me, *that* was where it had all begun, so to speak, even if that wasn't the case. "Or the place where you were born?"

"I was born in the château, and I temporarily took the king's dragon in the backyard of the same château." Thorn took a sip of soup. "He wouldn't risk doing this too close to home. He doesn't want anyone to realize you were taken. So...the next logical place is where I was *supposed* to die. It's where Falkor also told me to go."

I wasn't sure if that could be considered the beginning, but it was the place that marked the start of Thorn's new life. Maybe that was why Drake had thought of it.

"Château, eh?" I lightened my tone. "Sounds fancy." I lifted my glass, extending my pinky.

He laughed, the sound soothing like a brush stroke. "It is. *Mansion* doesn't convey royalty, but we can't use the term *palace* for fear of humans overhearing. So *château* is the compromise."

"Is it in the heart of the dragon lands?" I set my glass down and grabbed the napkin by my plate. I wanted to learn everything about him, including his horrible past, if he was willing to tell me. Besides, I was a dragon shifter, which meant Drake and King Arman were my leaders.

He nodded. "It is, and it has the most acreage of any dragon property. The servants' homes are on part of the thousand acres, and the woods take up over half the space."

Licking my lips, I tried to fight off fatigue. "Are the homes all lumped together in one section, or do they have woods between them?"

Putting down his spoon, he leaned back in his chair and observed me. "They're clustered together so that the woods are wide open. Why?"

"I want to get an idea of what we're up against. If we're going to rescue them, I need to know how the area is laid out." I took a deep, calming breath to steady my heartbeat.

"Let's talk about it after we sleep." He placed a hand on mine. "We'll figure out a way to save all three of them tomorrow. I *promise*."

That was the thing: I wasn't sure he could make that promise. "What if we can't?"

"Vlad and Cass spent half their lives evading the royal guard and staying off the radar. If ever three dragons had a chance to escape, it's them. Besides, there's no way in *hell* we're handing you over." Thorn shook his head. "I don't care about the consequences. You have a lifetime of happiness ahead of you."

What he wasn't saying was telling. "What about you? You're only talking about me. If you're turning yourself in, there's no way in hell I'm staying behind."

He pinched the bridge of his nose and hung his head. "My parents made me swear that if they got captured, I wouldn't risk myself to save them. I had no intention of keeping that promise, but if it's the only way to keep you safe—" His turmoil swirled between us like a raging tornado.

My heart fractured from his pain as his love flowed into me, taking me by surprise. He was contemplating *sacrificing his parents* for me. "Thorn—"

"Look, let's take a moment to enjoy each other's company." He squeezed my hand gently. "We'll strategize a way to save them all. But Ev, you're the most important thing to me. A precious gem that sparkles through the night, giving me my first sense of peace since I was a young boy. I can't lose you. I *won't*."

The way his irises glowed as he locked gazes with me informed me of his resolve. I couldn't talk him out of this. However, I also knew what it was like to lose a parent. It shredded your soul in ways you couldn't imagine. And every day, as their voice and laughter faded from memory, part of you went along with it.

If I gave myself up to Drake, even if Thorn and I couldn't be together, at least his parents and I would all be alive, and he would survive. But there was no way I could convince him of that, and I feared that if he chose me over his parents, he'd grow to resent me as we got older. "I want you to be happy, too. I can't lose you, either."

"I am happy and will be forever, as long as we're together." He smiled adoringly.

I leaned over and kissed his lips. "I can agree to that." He was right about one thing: the three of them were dragons. If he believed that much in Vlad and Cassidy, I would, too.

His body relaxed. "I'll go shower. Why don't you get ready for bed? Then we can get some rest."

"Okay." I smiled, scanning his chiseled face. The existence of someone so gorgeous shouldn't have been possible, yet here he was...my *mate*. My dragon purred.

He stood from the table and picked up his plate.

"Hey, you cooked. I'll clean." I clasped his wrist. "It's only fair." I'd never had someone take care of me the way he did, and the last thing I wanted to do was take advantage.

"But—" he started.

"Seriously. I'd like to take care of you, too, so let me do it from time to time." My cheeks hurt from smiling again. The sensation used to be foreign to me. "Forever is a long time for me to sit around. I need to stay limber."

He winked. "You just took care of me in the bedroom. *That* you can do any time you want."

My body heated with desire, and he grinned like a dragon that ate a cat that ate the canary.

Nope. He was getting too big of a head already. "Just go. I'll clean up."

"Fine, but tomorrow, you'll be punished for back talking," he said, brushing past me so my arm touched his groin.

Unable to resist, I watched his ass as he strolled from the kitchen and out of view.

He might be the death of me.

Once he disappeared, my gaze landed on my phone. It should have enough juice for me to turn it on and see if the twins had tried to reach me. Eva had actually looked distraught when I'd left. I took my last bite of grilled cheese, then walked over and powered it up.

As soon as the phone cycled through the welcome, my phone dinged with text messages. Several were from Eva.

The shower turned on in the bathroom as I read through them all. She was concerned, asking me why I wasn't answering. The last text read, **Please call me ASAP.**

She'd never asked me to call before.

The shower curtain closed as Thorn got into the shower. I hit the call button.

She picked up on the first ring. "Everly?" Her voice was thick with tears. "Is it really you?"

My lungs seized. "Yes. What's wrong?"

"I've been kidnapped," she breathed as a sob racked her body. "Drake took me."

The walls closed in on me, and my vision darkened around the edges. "Is he there with you?"

"Yes, him and a girl named Saphira," she answered.

A dark chuckle echoed from the other side of the line, followed by Drake saying, "Tell your sister that if she doesn't want you to take her place, she has to turn herself over."

Eva whimpered. "He said—"

I wouldn't force her to repeat that. "I can hear him."

"Oh, that's right. She's a *dragon* now," he growled.

It sounded as if Eva was hyperventilating, and my heart squeezed.

"If you hurt her—" I started.

"If you don't want your sister to become my personal breeder, I expect you to return to me within two hours. I'll even sweeten the deal. If you hand yourself over in that time, I'll release your sister, Saphira, *and* Thorn's parents. You have my word."

Razor-sharp pain slid through my entire chest, as if my saliva had turned into a weapon.

Babe, what's wrong? Thorn connected.

He had to be feeling my turmoil like I'd felt his. *Just stressed.*

"Everly, you can trust his word this time," Saphira said. "He has witnesses, so he can't go back on it."

She knew how desperate I was to protect my sister, but she didn't realize I would have to give up my fated mate to save her.

CHAPTER TWENTY-SIX

MY BREATH CAUGHT, and the water from the shower turned off. I'd run out of time.

Eva started sobbing, and my entire world crumbled. "Fine." The word felt like sandpaper rubbing my throat raw.

"Aw, the love you have for family. It's endearing. Continue straight past where you met Brenton, and you'll find the château. It's two connected houses. Then fly south. You'll find us." His voice grew louder as he took the phone. "Two hours." The line went dead.

I stared at my phone, wondering what the hell had happened. But this solution would not only save my sister but Saphira and Thorn's parents as well. This was the best option, and it had to happen tonight.

My mind raced. Thorn and I were exhausted from the long night, the flight, and completing our bond. I'd barely been able to keep my eyes open...until now. I couldn't sleep, knowing I had to find a way out of here without alerting Thorn.

I promise it'll be okay, Thorn connected as his footsteps drew closer. *Where are you? I thought you'd already be in bed.*

I placed the phone back onto the table, making sure the screen was off. I didn't need him to notice anything out of the ordinary. I quietly climbed to my feet and cleared the table. *Sorry, I finished eating and was tidying up.*

He entered the living room and kitchen as I placed the plates, bowls, and cups into the sink.

I turned and stared at him. He was more gorgeous than any painting or sculpture I'd ever seen. His hair was wet and hung across his forehead, his sky blue irises sparkling. He wore dark gray pajama pants, but even through them I could see his *outline,* and even better, he was shirtless. His wide, muscular chest was on full display, his six-pack begging me to touch it.

"I know you want to clean up, but this can wait a couple of hours so we can get some rest," he said through a yawn. He took my hands and led me toward the bedroom.

The bolts of electricity sizzling between us stole my breath, but I managed to quirk a brow. "Are you putting me back into the room I shared with Saphira?"

"Nope." He grinned wickedly. "I want your dragon to come out and play whenever she wants."

My heart fluttered as he picked me up like a princess and carried me the rest of the way before laying me down on the bed, which now had lavender sheets. He kissed me and connected, *Besides, this is our room now. We share everything.*

That was like a punch to the gut. He might be sharing everything, but as of five minutes ago, I was not. My dragon grunted, but she didn't roar in anger. I realized she was just as desperate as I was to protect our mate emotionally. I replied in the most honest way I could. *I love you.*

He scooted me over and crawled into the spot beside me. He wrapped his arms around me, and I felt safe and cared for. Tears burned my eyes. I'd never felt anything like this before—hadn't felt protected in forever.

"Hey, I love you, too," he murmured and wiped the tears off my cheeks. "What's wrong?"

So much. I knew I'd never feel this serenity again. As soon as I'd found it, I had to lose it. But *he* was worth it. I'd rather him hate me than himself. I forced a smile. "You make me so *damn* happy."

"Well, I don't want to be the reason you cry, even if they're happy tears." He tightened his arms. "My life's goal is to make you smile as much as possible and protect you."

He couldn't have said more perfect words.

Needing to taste him again, I kissed him. When he responded, I tried to deepen the kiss, wanting to make love with him one more time.

He pulled back. "Babe, I want you so damn bad. Don't make this any harder."

A smile spread across my face. "That's kinda the point. I want to make you harder."

"Naughty girl," he chuckled, warmth spreading through our bond. "But my desire for you is only outweighed by my love. You need time to heal, which means you need rest. When we wake up in a few hours, I'll let you ravish me."

My body tensed. There wouldn't be a next time, but if I pushed, he'd know something was up. "Okay, but one more kiss?"

He kissed me, his tongue swooping into my mouth. I closed my eyes, relishing each touch, stroke, and sizzle that soared between us. When my fingers brushed the curves of his stomach, he shuddered and ended our kiss.

"I know what you're up to, and it's not happening. We aren't in a rush. We have the rest of our lives to have tons of sex." He kissed my nose. "Sleep before I have to handcuff you to the headboard."

He was teasing, but I didn't want to take the chance, especially since I needed to get out of here.

"Fine," I huffed, which caused his shoulders to shake.

Goodnight, my love, he connected as he breathed in my hair.

A sob built in my chest, but I swallowed it down. *Goodnight, Thorn.* I *wanted* to say more, but I couldn't.

I had no doubt that by the way Drake had worded his reply, if I waited too long, he'd rescind the offer. I couldn't risk Thorn's parents, Saphira, or my sister. Most importantly, I couldn't risk Thorn. I believed if it came down to it and we didn't find another solution, he'd give himself up to save them all. The difference between him and me doing it was that my way kept Thorn alive. If he turned himself in, the king would kill him.

I lay still in the arms of the man who now owned me, heart and soul, and listened to his steady heartbeat and the sound of air filling and leaving his lungs.

All too soon, his heart rate slowed, and his breathing steadied. Our connection cooled, indicating it would soon be time for me to make my move. I waited a few more minutes, then wiggled as if to get comfortable. I murmured, "So hot," as if that would make a difference.

He immediately released me, despite being sound asleep, and scooted over half an inch. Close enough that the electricity pulsed between us but far enough away that the cool air hit me.

Even in his sleep, he was taking care of me.

My heart shredded, the pain worse than anything I'd experienced before, and my body ached for his warmth. But I had to remember why I was doing this—for him.

I inched out of bed, the mattress barely shifting. Becoming a dragon had made me a lot more graceful. When I placed a foot on the cool wooden floor, my ankle nearly gave out. I balanced myself on the mattress, causing it to bounce, and steadied myself before my ass hit the floor and made a ton of commotion.

Maybe there was a higher power, fate or karma, making sure I stayed grounded, literally and figuratively.

His eyelids fluttered, and I whispered, "Hey. Sorry. I'm just getting a drink of water."

Hurry back, he connected and closed his eyes.

Not wanting to lie and wake him further, I tiptoed from the bedroom toward the living room and kitchen. I went directly to the sink and turned on the faucet. I had to at least pretend I was doing what I'd said. Our connection cooled again, and he fell deeper asleep.

Using the sound of the water, I strolled to the window in front of the kitchen table, which overlooked the side of the yard. I unlocked the latch and eased the window up so it didn't make any noise. When it was halfway up, the opening was large enough for me to fit through.

Needing to keep up the illusion, I went back to the sink and turned the water off. Our bond was still cool, but I suspected it wouldn't stay that way for long.

I had to go.

I rushed past the kitchen table and slipped out the window. Once my feet hit the ground, I ran as quickly as possible toward the tree line we'd come through earlier. The night sky was lightening, hinting that the sun would rise soon.

When I reached the trees, I quickly undressed, and my dragon surged forward. I didn't even have to ask, and I hoped that meant we were growing more in sync. I tried to pick up my clothes with my talons but couldn't grab them.

Damn big dragon hands. I tried again more slowly and snagged them.

Soon, I was flying high in the sky toward the dragon homestead. From Drake's directions, I should be able to find the château. If his arrogance was any indication, it wouldn't be hard to miss.

Each flap of wings that took me farther from Thorn broke my heart. I tamped down my emotions, not wanting to alert him to what was going on. If he found out too soon, he could stop me, so I had to keep a level head. I'd heard that people could die of a broken heart, but I'd never believed it. Science didn't support that theory, but I feared I was about to learn how wrong I'd been before I even made it to Drake. I hadn't believed anyone could feel the sort of torture now ravaging my soul.

My dragon's pain blended with mine. The separation of animal and human blurred more every time I shifted into dragon form. Maybe that was why dragon magic made dragons shift so often—to ensure they didn't become separate beings like we'd been before I shifted.

That was something I could research and focus on later once my future as Drake's property began.

All too soon, I passed the place where we'd met Brenton, the very person who'd betrayed us when we'd foolishly hoped we could save everyone without losing anything. I forced myself to look elsewhere, not wanting to feel the stab of betrayal all over again.

I took a deep breath to regulate my emotions. I had to be strong; otherwise, Thorn would know exactly where to find me, and I needed him to stay asleep for as long as possible.

Following Drake's instructions, I passed over the houses. They started out small but soon became bigger. I was getting closer to the château.

After a few more minutes, I flew over a huge mansion that looked like two connected homes. The gigantic house was sunflower yellow with gray trim and a beige roof that slanted down into a sizable terrace in front of an immaculate green backyard.

My stomach clenched. That had to be where Thorn had been playing tag with the king when the incident had happened. An accident where an innocent, sweet boy's life had changed due to fear.

My connection to Thorn warmed in my chest, surprising me. I'd lost focus on staying level-headed as I'd searched for Drake and the others. Even in dragon form, my eyes burned with unshed tears.

Ev? Thorn connected.

My breath sawed through my lungs in a gasp. I wasn't sure how to respond. I hadn't reached Drake yet.

Flying lower, I entered the woods behind the château. I'd be there soon.

Why aren't you back in bed yet? Thorn asked. *Why are you upset? What's wrong?*

I'd been gone only thirty minutes, and he was already awake and searching for me. I'd hoped his parents would be on their way to him before he realized I'd left. *Thorn, I'm sorry.*

Warmth spread through me as he replied, *Babe. Nothing to be sorry about. Just come back to bed before I make you.*

My heart stuttered just as Drake, Eva, Saphira, and two people I'd never seen before came into view.

Eva's steel blue eyes bulged with fear, and her long, dark brown hair was messy. She wore her favorite sleep outfit—a heather gray shirt that said *OMG aRe YoU a GIRL GaMeR?* in purple, with a purple controller underneath, and matching purple plaid bottoms. It had been her Christmas present from Elliott last year.

The strange man had greasy caramel hair plastered to his face, his ivory skin so pale it appeared ghostly. His cornflower eyes looked sunken, but the way they widened as he watched me approach made my blood run cold. The woman's golden brown hair hung limply past her shoulders, her tanned skin splotchy as if she hadn't been eating well, and her hazel eyes were dark with pain.

They had to be Thorn's parents. Just like Saphira, they each had a collar locked around their necks.

Drake's dark gaze was already fixed on me, and cold fear spiraled through my gut.

What's wrong? Thorn asked as alarm rang through our bond. *Ev, where the fuck are you?* Hot anger and icy fear followed the alarm.

He already knew, so I didn't need to tell him. Instead, I said, *Drake had Eva contact me. He kidnapped her and threatened to use her as his breeder if I didn't turn myself in tonight. He promised to release not only her but Saphira and your parents. My life for four. I know what it's like to lose a parent, and if there'd been a way I could've saved my mom and didn't, I wouldn't have been able to live with myself.*

Everly, get your ass back here right now. *You can't trust him,* Thorn commanded. *I'll be fine just as long as you're by my side. We'll figure this out together. I can't live without you.*

Saphira told me his word is good because there are witnesses. This is how I can save all four of them. I had to do it. You think risking me is too great of a cost, but... What was left of my heart shattered. *I'd rather you hate me than yourself.*

He lies, Everly. He'll do anything to get you there. And I could never *hate you. None of this is your fault. Besides, don't you realize I'll just come after you?* His love surged through our bond. *If you don't know that, you clearly didn't think this through.*

My heart ached. *I can't risk you dying. Nothing is worth that.*

And nothing is worth losing you. His determination slammed into me, stealing my breath. *Now turn around and come home to me.*

Home.

Thorn was my home. I hadn't realized that was how I felt about him.

Everything inside me wanted to head *home,* but I couldn't. *I'm already here.*

His dragon's roar echoed in my head as I landed in front of Drake, my attention locked on my sister, who was shaking so hard, her teeth chattered.

My dragon form had to be taking my emotions over the top. I lifted the talon that held my clothes and nodded toward a section of thicker trees.

"I shall allow it." Drake's attention flicked to the tree line, where I sensed ten guards scattered about. "Jessie, go with her and keep an eye on her as she shifts back. If one of the men even glances at her while she's naked, kill him on the spot."

He wasn't protecting me; he just didn't want anyone to see his property nude. I didn't bother waiting, just turned and headed for the trees. Jessie stepped out from my left and followed me as I headed to the right.

If he touches you, his death will be slow and painful, Thorn connected as his boiling rage swirled inside me.

That should have scared me, but his words thrilled me.

In the trees, my dragon receded, and I was back in human form. I dressed, trying to become logical. *Thorn, if you come here, they'll kill you. You'll be outnumbered. Don't. If you're determined, wait until your parents come back, and plan something with them.*

I'm coming for you, he replied. *Waiting is not an option.*

I turned to find Jessie with her hand on her rifle, but I ignored her. I needed to get out there and make sure all four prisoners were released. I knew Thorn's parents wouldn't let him do something this risky.

I marched past her and back into the small clearing. Thorn's parents and Saphira were still collared, and Eva had her arms wrapped around her.

"I'm here. Release the four of them like you promised." I marched until I stood a few feet in front of Drake.

"Everly?" Eva gasped. "When did you get here?"

Stupidly, I hadn't been prepared for this question. Of course she didn't know I was a dragon shifter. I'd been so focused on Thorn that I hadn't realized my sister would learn what I'd become. "Just now."

Drake laughed cruelly. "She's the dragon that appeared not five minutes ago."

"It's true?" Eva's face blanched. "*You're* one of them? No."

A sour taste filled my mouth, but there was no time for me to address her reaction, and I refused to let Drake watch this exchange. I glared at him.

He lifted his chin, staring down his nose at me. "You do realize I'm the one in control here? Not the other way around."

Games. He loved playing them, but I was tired and not in the mood. I needed him to release Thorn's parents. "You promised that if I came here, you would let the four of them go."

"I did. You're right." He tapped his finger to his mouth. "But...I changed my mind." He sneered, his dark eyes glowing.

My vision blurred. "I came here within two hours as agreed. You can't renege."

"That's the thing, Everly. I never had any intention of releasing any of them." He walked a few steps closer and sniffed me. "I said it to get you here, but *this* is a surprise. Not only did you somehow become a dragon shifter, but you also *mated* with someone."

My world tilted, and I glanced at Saphira. "You swore he'd keep his word."

Saphira nodded, her jaw clenching. "I heard him agree to it. Drake has to let us go."

"Stupid women." Drake rolled his eyes. "I'm the king's heir. Those laws don't apply to me. I can do whatever *I* want. I am the *law*."

"If King Arman—" Cassidy started.

Drake cut her off with loud laughter. "My father

won't do anything to me. I'm the golden son. So shut your mouth, or your death will be imminent."

"Don't you *dare* talk to her like that," Vlad snapped, seething.

"Or what?" Drake lifted his arms. "You can't do anything."

This situation was growing worse by the second. "Fine," I said. "If you won't honor that agreement, then honor the first. Let Eva go."

"No." Drake's irises darkened. "You're a dragon, and I need a human breeder. But now I have something else that the abomination will do anything for—*you*. This is a bonus." He leaned into my face. "My plans were to capture his parents and hope that he came, but with his fated mate in my power, there's no question he'll come."

When I flinched, I heard him inhale as if he were absorbing all my disgust and fear.

Thorn, the king didn't capture your parents, I hastily linked. *It was Drake.*

What? Thorn's shock registered, then turned into disgust. *He'll regret ever being born.*

"You've been given a new role," Drake whispered, his breath hitting my ear. "My wife. And your sister will be my breeder. We'll be one happy family, especially once I kill Saphira, Cassidy, Vlad, and the abomination."

My legs wobbled, but I forced myself to remain upright. I wouldn't crumble in front of him. *I'm sorry. I fucked up. He won't let any of them go.*

"Half of you, take my prisoners back to their hiding spot. We'll execute them in twenty-four hours, hopefully with the abomination in tow." Drake flicked his hand at the guards. "And half of you, take my *future wife* and *breeder* to the guest portion of the château. I'll make my father aware that we'll be organizing my wedding in the morning."

The guards came as ordered. Saphira, Vlad, and Cassidy stood there, waiting to be escorted away. They didn't fight, cry, or beg but remained calm and collected. I suspected they were biding their time.

Falkor strolled to my sister and pointed at the château.

Tears poured down my sister's face. "No, please. Let me go."

Black dots obstructed my vision as my heart thrashed in my ears. I had come here to prevent this, but instead, I'd made things worse.

Thorn would fly right into their hands.

My knees gave out, and I dropped to the ground.

There wasn't a damn thing I could do to protect any of them. I'd broken my promise to Mom, and I'd ripped my own heart to shreds by foolishly leaving Thorn behind.

With cold tendrils of fear weaving through me and binding my chest, I realized I had led my fated mate to his death.

ABOUT THE AUTHOR

Jen L. Grey is a *USA Today* Bestselling Author who writes Paranormal Romance, Urban Fantasy, and Fantasy genres.

Jen lives in Tennessee with her husband, two daughters, and two miniature Australian Shepherds. Before she began writing, she was an avid reader and enjoyed being involved in the indie community. Her love for books eventually led her to writing. For more information, please visit her website and sign up for her newsletter.

Check out her future projects and book signing events at her website.
www.jenlgrey.com

ALSO BY JEN L. GREY

The Marked Dragon Prince Trilogy

Ruthless Mate

Marked Dragon

Hidden Fate

Shadow City: Silver Wolf Trilogy

Broken Mate

Rising Darkness

Silver Moon

Shadow City: Royal Vampire Trilogy

Cursed Mate

Shadow Bitten

Demon Blood

Shadow City: Demon Wolf Trilogy

Ruined Mate

Shattered Curse

Fated Souls

Shadow City: Dark Angel Trilogy

Fallen Mate

Demon Marked

Dark Prince

Fatal Secrets

Shadow City: Silver Mate

Shattered Wolf

Fated Hearts

Ruthless Moon

The Wolf Born Trilogy

Hidden Mate

Blood Secrets

Awakened Magic

The Hidden King Trilogy

Dragon Mate

Dragon Heir

Dragon Queen

The Marked Wolf Trilogy

Moon Kissed

Chosen Wolf

Broken Curse

Wolf Moon Academy Trilogy

Shadow Mate

Blood Legacy

Rising Fate

The Royal Heir Trilogy

Wolves' Queen

Wolf Unleashed

Wolf's Claim

Bloodshed Academy Trilogy

Year One

Year Two

Year Three

The Half-Breed Prison Duology (Same World As Bloodshed Academy)

Hunted

Cursed

The Artifact Reaper Series

Reaper: The Beginning

Reaper of Earth

Reaper of Wings

Reaper of Flames

Reaper of Water

Stones of Amaria (Shared World)

Kingdom of Storms

Kingdom of Shadows

Kingdom of Ruins

Kingdom of Fire

The Pearson Prophecy

Dawning Ascent

Enlightened Ascent

Reigning Ascent

Stand Alones

Death's Angel

Rising Alpha